Beyond The Stars

Galactic Nexus Series, Volume 1

Anupam Roy

Published by Anupam Roy, 2024.

This is a work of fiction. Similarities to real people, places, or events are entirely coincidental.

BEYOND THE STARS

First edition. November 2, 2024.

Copyright © 2024 Anupam Roy.

ISBN: 979-8224786992

Written by Anupam Roy.

Table of Contents

Preface 1
Chapter 1: The City of Tomorrow 3
Chapter 2: A Glimpse of Interplanetary Life 7
Chapter 3: Meeting Rosy 13
Chapter 4: The University Project 19
Chapter 5: First Adventure Beyond Earth 25
Chapter 6: Exploration and Realization 31
Chapter 7: A Journey to the Moon 37
Chapter 8: Uncovering the Scheme 43
Chapter 9: The Chase Begins 49
Chapter 10: Digging Deeper 53
Chapter 11: Into Dangerous Waters 57
Chapter 12: The Revelation 63
Chapter 13: The Threat Revealed 69
Chapter 14: A Narrow Escape 73
Chapter 15: The Decision to Act 77
Chapter 16: Unconventional Allies 83
Chapter 17: The Heart of the Network 87
Chapter 18: Strength in Unity 93
Chapter 19: The Mars Mission 99
Chapter 20: Creating the Diversion 103
Chapter 21: The Evidence and Escape 109
Chapter 22: Captured 113
Chapter 23: Face to Face with the Enemy 117
Chapter 24: Escape in the Chaos 123
Chapter 25: A Desperate Signal 129
Chapter 26: Robusco's Arrival 135
Chapter 27: The Final Stand 141
Chapter 28: The Last Gambit 147
Chapter 29: A Hero's Welcome 153
Chapter 30: A New Beginning 157

Preface

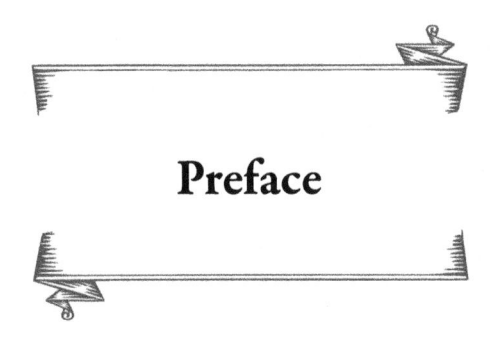

In the year 3200, humanity has redefined itself. With technology beyond what anyone once imagined, societies across Earth and its neighboring planets thrive in a vast interconnected universe, moving seamlessly between worlds, sharing knowledge, resources, and ambitions. Distances have shrunk, travel has become swift, and communications instantaneous. Yet, despite these advancements, certain forces still linger in the shadows, exploiting technology and commerce for their gain.

This is the world Jack, a young university student with a curiosity that matches his drive, inhabits. Growing up on Earth, Jack has spent his life captivated by the stars and the unknown. His passion for discovery leads him to new places, new faces, and ultimately, new challenges that push him far beyond what he could ever have expected.

When he meets Rosy—a brilliant, adventurous soul as eager to explore the cosmos as he is—Jack's path takes a thrilling turn. Together, they find themselves entangled in a perilous web of crime, smuggling, and deception led by a mysterious figure named Robusco, who operates a sprawling empire across the solar system. Their journey to expose his dark network becomes more than a mission; it becomes a battle of survival, courage, and resilience.

Beyond the Stars is a tale of discovery, friendship, and love, set against a cosmic backdrop that tests the limits of human spirit and connection. Jack and Rosy's journey reminds us that even in a world as advanced as ours, some things—courage, loyalty, and hope—are

ANUPAM ROY

timeless. As they push through adversities both vast and intimate, they become more than just a young couple fighting for justice; they become a beacon of inspiration for all who look beyond the stars in search of something greater.

This is their story. And it's only the beginning.

Happy Reading!

Anupam Roy

Chapter 1: The City of Tomorrow

Jack's eyes fluttered open to the soft hum of his alarm. It wasn't a jarring sound but a gentle melody that eased him out of sleep, programmed to match his circadian rhythm. Sunlight streamed into his room through windows that automatically adjusted their tint to let in just the right amount of morning glow. His apartment was sleek, minimalist, and modern, with smooth, curved surfaces and soft lighting.

As he sat up, a voice spoke out, crisp and clear. "Good morning, Jack. It's 7:30 AM. Your first class starts in an hour. Breakfast is ready."

Jack rubbed his eyes and smiled. "Thanks, Aira." The voice belonged to Aira, his virtual assistant. Embedded in his wristwatch, she managed everything from reminders to daily tasks, making sure Jack's life ran smoothly.

He stepped out of bed and into the shower, where water misted around him, adjusting to his preferred temperature. As he washed up, he could hear Aira's voice echoing softly through the bathroom. "Today's forecast is clear skies, with mild temperatures. You have a lecture on interstellar navigation, followed by a project meeting. Would you like me to run through the rest of your schedule?"

"Not now, Aira. Just play some music," Jack replied.

The shower filled with a soothing, rhythmic beat, and Jack relaxed under the warm spray. Once he was done, he stepped out and was greeted by the scent of freshly brewed coffee and toasted bread. His breakfast was already laid out on the dining table, courtesy of his automated kitchen system. Jack grabbed a piece of toast, took a bite, and let his mind wander as he sipped his coffee.

He gazed out the window at the bustling city below. *Skyreach*, as it was called, was a testament to how far humanity had come. Skyscrapers stretched high into the sky, their surfaces gleaming under the morning sun. Flying vehicles zipped through the air, following precise, invisible paths, and high-speed pods darted along the ground, weaving between pedestrians who strolled through lush green parks scattered throughout the city. Despite the futuristic look, there was a sense of calm and order, a peaceful hum that made everything feel connected.

Jack finished his breakfast and grabbed his backpack, slinging it over his shoulder. "Aira, let's head out."

As he stepped out of his apartment, the door slid shut behind him, locking automatically. He made his way to the nearest *transit hub*, a streamlined structure where people boarded high-speed pods that would whisk them away to their destinations. Jack loved this part of his morning. The pods were efficient, quiet, and quick, and watching the city blur past through the pod's clear glass always gave him a rush.

The transit hub was buzzing with activity as usual. Robots clad in sleek, metallic exoskeletons moved around, assisting passengers, ensuring that the pods were operating smoothly, and handling any maintenance needs. Some robots even patrolled the area, their blue lights blinking gently, a reminder that law enforcement was always vigilant but unobtrusive.

Jack approached one of the waiting pods. "Destination: *Skyreach University, Main Campus*," he said, and the pod's door slid open. He stepped inside and took a seat, feeling the pod lurch softly as it began to accelerate.

As the pod glided through the city, Jack took a moment to appreciate the view. Tall, elegant towers stretched towards the sky, their surfaces reflecting the sunlight like polished gems. Between the buildings were stretches of greenery — parks, gardens, and even small

BEYOND THE STARS

lakes, offering residents a breath of nature amidst the urban sprawl. Automated drones zipped overhead, delivering packages, while people strolled along wide, open walkways, chatting, laughing, or simply enjoying the morning.

Soon, the pod slowed as it approached the university. The *Skyreach University* was a marvel in itself, a blend of glass, steel, and greenery. It looked less like a traditional campus and more like a futuristic oasis, with its botanical gardens, sky bridges, and open-air classrooms. Students from all over Earth — and even other planets — mingled in the sprawling courtyards, some reading under the shade of large, genetically-engineered trees, others discussing their projects in small groups.

Jack stepped out of the pod and joined the flow of students heading to their classes. He entered one of the main buildings, and as he made his way through the wide, brightly-lit hallways, he noticed the diversity around him. It wasn't just humans; there were people with slight differences in skin tone, eye shape, and even body structure, reflecting the small but growing communities that had settled on Mars, the Moon, and other celestial bodies. They all moved with a sense of purpose, yet there was a calm, almost serene atmosphere in the air.

Jack checked his wristwatch. *"Lecture on Space Exploration – Room 3A."* He quickened his pace, knowing he'd make it just in time.

As he entered the lecture hall, he was greeted by the sight of a humanoid AI standing at the front of the room. The professor, *Professor Solaris*, had a polished, metallic finish, and a face designed to be expressive yet neutral. His eyes glowed softly as he scanned the room, acknowledging each student as they walked in.

"Good morning, everyone," said Professor Solaris, his voice smooth and precise. "Today, we'll be continuing our discussion on the history of space exploration, focusing on humanity's first colonies beyond Earth."

Jack found a seat near the middle of the room and settled in, pulling out his tablet. The class began, and the lecture was accompanied by holographic displays that floated above the professor, showing images and videos from centuries past. From the first lunar colonies to the establishment of cities on Mars, the presentation was vivid and immersive, almost as if the students were traveling through time.

"As you know," continued Professor Solaris, "the development of superfast travel and communication was a turning point. It allowed humanity to thrive not just on Earth, but across the solar system. The interconnected nature of our society today is a result of these advancements."

Jack listened attentively. He had always been fascinated by the idea of space exploration. The thought of traveling to distant planets, seeing the stars up close, and understanding the mysteries of the universe had always thrilled him. As he watched a hologram depicting the construction of the first Martian city, he could feel a sense of pride and wonder. Humanity had come so far, and there was still so much more to explore.

As the lecture continued, Jack's tablet vibrated softly, and a message popped up. It was from *Sam*, one of his friends who was on Mars. "Hey, Jack! I just got back to Earth. Let's catch up after class?"

Jack smiled and quickly typed a response. "Sure thing, Sam. Meet you at the café in the quad."

The rest of the class went by quickly, and Jack found himself absorbed in the professor's explanations. By the time the lecture ended, he had jotted down several notes and felt even more inspired to pursue his studies. He gathered his things and headed out.

Chapter 2: A Glimpse of Interplanetary Life

Jack's day began with his usual brisk walk across the university's futuristic campus. The sun was high in the sky, casting warm, golden rays over the gleaming glass buildings and lush green courtyards. Today, Jack's schedule was packed, starting with a lecture on *Space Exploration* followed by classes on *interplanetary politics*, *robotics* and *astronomy*. Each subject painted a picture of how far humanity had come and hinted at where it might go next.

As he entered the sleek, silver-walled lecture hall, the room was already filled with holographic displays showing different planetary systems, their political structures, and complex trade routes. *Professor Zenith*, the AI who taught interplanetary politics, was already standing at the front, his metallic form glowing faintly. Today, his eyes pulsed with a cool blue, signaling the start of the lesson.

"Good morning, students," Professor Zenith said, his voice smooth and modulated, echoing slightly in the spacious room. "Today, we'll be discussing the political agreements that govern trade between Earth, Mars, and the other colonies. As you know, interplanetary relations are not just a matter of diplomacy, but also of economic and cultural exchange."

Jack slid into his seat, placing his tablet on the desk in front of him. Around him, other students from diverse backgrounds—some from Earth, others from lunar colonies, and a few from Mars—settled in, their expressions a mix of curiosity and anticipation.

Professor Zenith began with a holographic map of the solar system. Planets and moons hovered in the air, connected by bright, pulsing lines representing trade routes. As he spoke, the holograms shifted, zooming in on specific colonies, showing bustling spaceports and thriving cities.

"Earth may still be the most populous planet," Professor Zenith continued, "but Mars, Luna, and the Jovian moons have rapidly developed their own economies. Trade is the backbone of these colonies, and every day, thousands of ships traverse the solar system, carrying goods, resources, and even passengers between worlds."

Jack listened intently, taking notes as the professor explained how different planetary colonies specialized in various industries. Mars, with its vast terraforming efforts, had become the hub of agricultural research, while Luna, Earth's closest neighbor, was known for its advanced mining operations. Each colony was interdependent, creating a complex web of cooperation and mutual reliance.

As the lecture progressed, the room was filled with holographic visuals showing spaceports on Mars, with massive cargo ships unloading containers, and lunar miners working in the vast, dark caverns beneath the Moon's surface. It was hard not to be fascinated by how seamlessly humanity had managed to integrate itself across the stars.

The class was interactive, with students participating in discussions and simulations. At one point, Professor Zenith split them into groups and tasked them with solving a diplomatic scenario between a Martian agricultural colony and a lunar mining station. Jack found himself working with *Zara*, a student from Mars, and *Eli*, who had been born and raised on Luna.

"Okay, so if we're representing Mars," Jack said, leaning over the holographic table that displayed their scenario, "we need to figure out how to negotiate a better deal for importing lunar metals. Mars has the tech to terraform, but we need raw materials."

"Right," Zara nodded, tapping on the display to bring up more details. "But Luna controls the supply chain, so we have to offer something valuable in return. Maybe we can propose an exchange—agricultural products for raw metals?"

Eli, who had a mischievous grin, leaned back in her chair. "Or we could just undercut them and make a deal with Titan's traders instead," she suggested, half-jokingly.

The group laughed, and for a moment, it felt less like a classroom exercise and more like a genuine negotiation between representatives from different worlds. These simulations were one of the reasons Jack loved this class—it made him feel connected to the broader universe, beyond the confines of Earth.

The lesson concluded with a review of their solutions, and Professor Zenith provided feedback. "Remember, diplomacy is not just about power but about understanding what each side needs. Only then can you find a solution that benefits all."

Jack left the lecture hall feeling energized. The discussions were intense but engaging, and it was clear that the future of interplanetary relations was in the hands of young minds like his. He checked his wristwatch, noting that he had about ten minutes before his robotics class started.

The rest of his morning passed quickly. In *robotics*, they were working on building automated assistants, a project that fascinated Jack. He and his classmates designed programs to make the robots more intuitive and responsive, experimenting with different algorithms. The class was guided by *Professor Orion*, another AI who had a subtle wit that kept everyone engaged.

"You'll find that programming robots is much like training a pet," Professor Orion said, as a small spherical drone floated around him, responding to his commands. "You have to be precise, but also patient. Remember, they can only learn what you teach them."

By the time Jack's final class, *astronomy*, ended, it was early afternoon. He walked out of the lecture hall, his mind buzzing with ideas and concepts from the day. He hadn't even realized how much he had learned until he stopped to take a breath, feeling the warm breeze against his face. The quad was alive with activity, students lounging on the grass, eating lunch, or just chatting with friends.

As he made his way to the nearby *transport hub*, Jack was eager to meet his friend *Sam*, who had just returned from Mars. The transport hub was a busy spot, with sleek, capsule-like pods arriving and departing, whisking passengers away to various parts of the city or even to the spaceports for interplanetary travel.

Jack found Sam waiting by a bench, looking out of place yet comfortable, his bright green jacket as eye-catching as ever.

"Hey!" Jack called out, waving as he approached. "How was Mars? Did you bring me back a Martian rock?"

Sam grinned, pushing himself off the bench. "Better than a rock, my friend. I've got stories. You wouldn't believe how much that place has changed since the last time I was there."

They headed to a nearby café, one of Jack's favorite spots on campus, and found a table by the window. As they sat down, Jack noticed how the café's AI servers moved fluidly between tables, taking orders, and delivering them with precision. It was all so seamless, like clockwork.

"So, how was Mars?" Jack asked as they waited for their drinks. "You were there for almost a month, right?"

"Yeah, and it was amazing," Sam said, leaning forward, his eyes bright with excitement. "The cities there... they've expanded so much. I remember the first time I went, everything felt so sparse, but now they've got these huge domes with artificial skies, parks, lakes, the works. It's like a mini Earth, but with red sand everywhere."

"Sounds like it's thriving," Jack said, intrigued. "What were you doing there, anyway?"

BEYOND THE STARS

"Just some business meetings. You know, trade stuff," Sam replied with a shrug. "But it's so routine now. You can just hop on a shuttle, and in a couple of hours, boom, you're on Mars. And it's cheap, too! I met this guy who commutes between Mars and Earth every week for work."

Jack raised an eyebrow, surprised. "Every week? I can't even imagine. I mean, it's not that far, but still."

"That's today's technology, my friend," Sam said, leaning back and stretching his arms. "Everything's connected now. It's not just Earth anymore. We're all part of this bigger, solar system-wide community."

Their drinks arrived, and as they sipped their coffee, they continued talking about the future and what it meant to be part of a universe that felt so much closer than ever before.

As the afternoon stretched on, Jack decided it was time to head back home. He said goodbye to Sam, promising to catch up again soon. On his way back to the transit hub, something caught his eye.

A girl, probably around his age, stood near the entrance of one of the university's main buildings, looking a bit lost. She had a warm smile, and there was a sense of curiosity in her eyes as she scanned her surroundings, trying to make sense of the bustling campus. Her hair was tied back in a simple ponytail, and she wore a jacket that had the emblem of *Lunar University* on it.

Jack hesitated for a moment. He thought about walking over and offering to help her find her way, but just as he was about to take a step, she pulled out her tablet and seemed to figure things out on her own. She gave a small nod, as if confirming something, and then disappeared into the crowd.

Jack watched her go, feeling a strange sense of curiosity. Who was she? A new student, perhaps? He shrugged, figuring he'd see her around again. There was something about her smile that stayed with him, though, even as he boarded the pod back to his apartment.

The pod sped through the city, and Jack leaned back, his mind still wandering. The day had been filled with insights and experiences, from discussions on politics to Sam's stories about Mars. But the image of the girl with the warm smile lingered, a tiny, unanswered question that he hoped would find an answer soon.

As the city lights blurred past, Jack felt a strange sense of anticipation. The universe was vast, and the future was wide open. And somehow, he felt that the girl he had seen was going to be a part of it.

Chapter 3: Meeting Rosy

The next morning, Jack found himself distracted. As he sat in his robotics class, listening to Professor Orion explain the intricacies of autonomous drone programming, his thoughts kept drifting back to the girl he had seen near the university's main building the day before. Who was she? What brought her to Earth? There was something about her that had captured his attention, and he couldn't quite place why.

"Jack, would you care to demonstrate how the drone's navigation protocol functions?" Professor Orion's voice snapped him back to reality.

"Oh, uh, sure, Professor," Jack stammered, quickly adjusting the control panel on his tablet. He activated a small spherical drone, guiding it to float smoothly around the room, weaving between desks and students. The class clapped politely as the demonstration ended, and Jack managed a sheepish smile.

"Thank you, Jack. That was... adequate," Professor Orion said, his robotic tone infused with just the slightest hint of amusement. "Perhaps next time, a little more focus?"

Jack chuckled along with the class, but his mind was still elsewhere. As the lecture ended and the students began packing up, he decided that if he saw the girl again today, he wouldn't let the opportunity pass. He'd introduce himself. He felt oddly determined, as if something important was about to happen, and he didn't want to miss it.

The day passed by in a blur of classes. In interplanetary politics, Jack was paired with Zara and Eli again to analyze trade policies between

Earth and Titan. Later, in astronomy, Professor Nebula—a sleek, silver robot with an elegant, ethereal design—guided them through a simulation of the Milky Way, showing how gravitational forces shaped the galaxy. Normally, Jack would have been fascinated, but today he found it hard to concentrate.

Finally, during a break between his classes, he decided to head to the university's *virtual library* to catch up on some reading. The library was a marvel, with holographic bookshelves stretching endlessly, each shelf filled with millions of digitized books, research papers, and educational programs. You could access almost any piece of knowledge ever recorded with just a few taps on a screen.

As Jack entered the library, he spotted her almost immediately. She was standing by one of the large, interactive displays, her brow furrowed as she struggled to navigate the system. She tapped the screen a few times, then crossed her arms, clearly frustrated.

Jack felt a rush of excitement. This was his chance. He walked over, trying to look casual. "Hey, need some help?" he asked, giving her a friendly smile.

The girl turned, and for a moment, she looked surprised. Then, her expression softened, and she smiled back. "Oh, hi! Yeah, I'm… kind of lost here. I'm trying to find some papers on bioengineering, but I think I've opened a dozen windows, and none of them are what I need."

Jack glanced at the screen, which was indeed cluttered with open tabs and search results that had nothing to do with bioengineering. He chuckled. "Yeah, the system can be a bit tricky at first. Here, let me show you."

He reached over and tapped a few buttons, quickly clearing the screen. Then, he brought up the search menu and entered a few keywords. Almost instantly, the display organized itself, showing a neat list of relevant articles and books. "There you go," he said. "It's all about knowing how to talk to it."

BEYOND THE STARS

The girl's eyes lit up as she looked at the screen. "Wow, that's... way easier than what I was trying to do. Thank you so much! I'm still getting used to all this." She turned to him, extending her hand. "I'm Rosy, by the way."

"Jack," he said, shaking her hand. "Nice to meet you, Rosy. Are you new here?"

She nodded. "Yeah, I just transferred from Lunar University. It's my first week, and I'm still figuring things out. Everything here is so... different."

"Lunar University?" Jack's eyes widened. "So, you're from the Moon?"

"Born and raised," she said with a laugh. "Well, mostly. My family moved there when I was little, so I've spent most of my life under a glass dome with an artificial sky. Coming to Earth has been a bit of a shock, to be honest. The real sky... it's so big."

Jack smiled. He could imagine how overwhelming it must be for someone who had lived under controlled, artificial environments all their life. "Yeah, it's a lot to take in. But you'll get used to it. And hey, if you need help figuring out the library or anything else, just ask."

Rosy's smile grew warmer. "Thanks, Jack. That's really kind of you. It's nice to meet someone who's not a robot, too."

Jack laughed. "Yeah, they're everywhere, aren't they? I mean, I like them, but sometimes it's nice to have a conversation that doesn't involve perfectly calculated responses."

Rosy nodded in agreement. "Exactly. At Lunar University, almost all the staff were robots, and they're great at teaching, but it's not the same as talking to a real person."

They continued chatting, and Jack found out that Rosy was majoring in *bioengineering*. She was passionate about genetic research and had come to Earth because she wanted to study under some of the best minds in the field. "There's so much more biodiversity here," she explained. "On the Moon, we have plants and animals, but everything is controlled. Here, it's wild and unpredictable, and that's what makes it exciting."

As they talked, Jack felt an easy connection with her. She was smart, curious, and had a way of speaking that made everything sound interesting. He decided to take a chance. "I could give you a tour of the campus, if you'd like," he offered. "There are some cool spots that aren't on the map. And I know this great place where you can get the best synthetic chocolate milkshake."

Rosy's eyes lit up. "That sounds amazing! I'd love a tour. And a chocolate milkshake sounds like just what I need."

They spent the next couple of hours walking around the campus. Jack showed her some of his favorite places, like the *botanical garden*, which was home to plants from all over the solar system, and the *student commons*, where people from different backgrounds gathered to chat, study, or play games. He even took her to the *rooftop observatory*, where telescopes pointed towards the sky, giving a clear view of the stars.

"This is where I come when I need to clear my head," Jack said as they stood by the railing, looking up at the sky. The sun was starting to set, and the first stars were beginning to appear, twinkling faintly against the darkening blue. "You can see everything from here. The city, the stars… it kind of makes you feel like you're a part of something bigger, you know?"

Rosy was quiet for a moment, taking it all in. "It's beautiful," she said softly. "I never thought I'd see the stars like this. On the Moon, they're always there, but you don't feel them the same way. Here… it feels real."

Jack glanced at her, noticing how the fading light caught in her eyes, making them shine. "I'm glad you like it. It's one of my favorite places."

They stayed there for a while, just talking. Rosy told Jack more about life on the Moon—how people lived in massive domes, with

BEYOND THE STARS

everything carefully controlled to mimic Earth's environment. She described the lunar nights, which lasted for weeks, and how she used to watch the Earth rise over the horizon, a tiny blue dot in the vast darkness.

Jack found it fascinating. "I've always wanted to visit the Moon," he said. "Maybe someday, when I'm not buried in assignments, I'll take a trip up there."

"You should," Rosy said. "I could be your tour guide this time. Show you all the best spots, like the *Sea of Tranquility* and the *Lunar Gardens*. And there's this one café in *New Tycho City* that makes the best steamed buns. I know it sounds weird, but they're really good."

Jack grinned. "It's a deal."

By the time they finished their tour, the campus was glowing with the soft lights of evening, and Jack felt like he had known Rosy for much longer than just a few hours. As they walked back towards the transport hub, he felt a pang of disappointment, knowing the day was coming to an end.

"So, how about that milkshake?" he asked, trying to keep the conversation going just a bit longer.

Rosy laughed. "You don't give up, do you? Alright, let's do it. But you're buying, since you're the one who suggested it."

"Fair enough," Jack said with a playful shrug. "Consider it a welcome-to-Earth gift."

They found the café, and Jack ordered two chocolate milkshakes. They sat by the window, watching people pass by, and talked about everything from their favorite books to their dreams for the future. By the end of the evening, Jack felt like he had made a real connection, and it was clear that Rosy felt the same.

As they said their goodbyes, Jack couldn't help but smile. "So, what do you think? Ready to explore more of Earth this weekend?"

Rosy's eyes sparkled with excitement. "Absolutely. I'm looking forward to it."

They exchanged numbers, and as Jack headed home, he realized that he hadn't thought about drones, politics, or even his classes all afternoon. Meeting Rosy had been a welcome surprise, and he couldn't wait to see where their new friendship would lead.

As he lay in bed that night, staring up at the ceiling, Jack thought about the way Rosy had looked at the stars, like she was seeing them for the first time. It made him realize that even though he had lived on Earth all his life, there were still so many things he took for granted. Maybe, with Rosy around, he'd start to see the world a little differently, too.

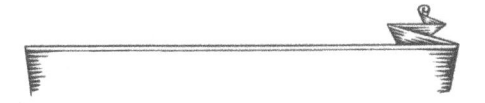

Chapter 4: The University Project

The university buzzed with its usual rhythm of activity—students hurriedly moving between classes, professors delivering lectures, and research assistants immersed in their experiments. Jack found himself more excited than usual as he made his way through the campus. He had just received the notification on his wristwatch: he'd been assigned to a new group project in his *Interplanetary Ecosystems* class, and his partner was Rosy.

He hadn't expected to see her name next to his. They had only known each other for a short time, but their recent interactions had already shown him that she was smart, curious, and eager to learn. Working on a project together would mean spending more time with her, and he couldn't help but smile at the thought.

He arrived at the university's *Eco-Research Lab*, a sleek, glass-walled building that housed all sorts of experiments related to planetary environments. The lab was bustling with activity, and Jack spotted Rosy at one of the workstations, already immersed in a holographic display. She looked up and waved as he approached, her face lighting up with a smile.

"Hey, partner!" she greeted. "Looks like we'll be spending a lot of time together."

"Hey, Rosy! I'm glad they paired us up. I was hoping I'd get someone who actually knows what they're doing," Jack joked, dropping his bag on the table beside her. "So, what's the plan?"

Rosy grinned. "I was just looking over the project brief. We're supposed to research how different planets have been made habitable for humans and what kind of technology is used to maintain those environments. It's pretty broad, but I think there's a lot of room to explore."

Jack nodded, already feeling ideas forming in his head. "Yeah, there's so much we could cover. Mars and its atmosphere domes, the floating cities of Venus, even the lunar greenhouses. Where should we start?"

Rosy pulled up a holographic display of their project outline, showing the major components they'd need to address: *atmospheric adaptation, temperature regulation, resource management,* and *biodiversity.* "I was thinking we could start by dividing up the research—maybe I could look into the biological aspects, like plant growth and genetic adaptation, and you could focus on the technological systems?"

Jack leaned back, considering it. "That makes sense. You're into bioengineering, right?"

"Yep, and I love it," she said, her eyes sparkling with enthusiasm. "I've always been fascinated by how life adapts to harsh conditions. I mean, look at Earth—life found a way to thrive in every environment imaginable. I want to figure out how to replicate that on other planets, maybe even make them more habitable than Earth."

Jack raised an eyebrow, impressed. "That's ambitious. I like it. I've always been more into the tech side—robots, drones, things like that. I guess I like solving problems by building things. But trying to understand how life adapts... that sounds pretty cool too."

They spent the next few hours brainstorming, their conversation flowing easily. Rosy pulled up various research papers and data sets, showing Jack some of the recent advances in *genetic engineering.* She explained how scientists were tweaking plant genes to make them more resilient, able to grow in the thin Martian atmosphere or survive the acidic clouds of Venus. Jack, in turn, showed her some of the latest developments in *terraforming technology*, like the use of automated drones to plant crops on Mars or the energy shields that protected the Venusian cities from harsh winds.

"So, did you always want to study this stuff?" Jack asked as they sifted through a particularly dense research article on atmospheric regulation.

Rosy nodded, a thoughtful expression on her face. "Yeah. Growing up on the Moon, you don't get to see a lot of green. Everything is controlled, artificial. I used to spend hours in the *Lunar Gardens*, just staring at the plants, trying to understand how they survived. That's when I knew I wanted to study bioengineering. I want to create life where there shouldn't be any."

Jack smiled. "That's really cool. I guess I'm kind of the opposite. I grew up surrounded by machines—my dad used to build drones for the *Interplanetary Transport Authority*, so I got to see all these amazing gadgets when I was a kid. I was always tinkering, trying to build my own stuff. I even built a mini-robot when I was ten... it didn't work, but it was still fun."

Rosy laughed. "I can totally see that. You're definitely the kind of person who'd try to build a robot army."

"Oh, absolutely," Jack said with a mock-serious nod. "But a friendly robot army. One that helps people."

"Well, if you ever need help with the 'friendly' part, let me know. I'll make sure they're programmed to be kind to plants too," Rosy teased.

As the day turned into evening, they found themselves still deep in conversation. The lab had emptied out, and they were the only ones left, surrounded by holographic screens displaying various models and data sets. They had already started drafting the outline of their project, dividing tasks and setting goals for what they wanted to accomplish over the next few weeks.

"I think this is going to be a great project," Jack said, glancing at the list of tasks they had come up with. "We've got a solid plan, and we're covering a lot of ground."

Rosy nodded, but then her expression softened. "You know, it's not just the project. I'm glad I get to do this with you, Jack. I didn't really know what to expect when I came here, and it's been a bit overwhelming. But meeting you... it's made everything a lot easier."

Jack felt a warmth spread through his chest at her words. "I feel the same way. I mean, I was just focused on getting through classes and building stuff, but meeting you has made everything... more interesting. I guess it's nice to have someone to share it with."

They both fell silent for a moment, and Jack realized just how comfortable he felt around Rosy. It was easy to talk to her, to share ideas, and even to joke around. He hadn't felt this connected to someone in a long time, and it was nice.

"So, same time tomorrow?" Rosy asked, breaking the silence.

"Definitely. Maybe we'll even make some real progress," Jack said with a grin.

"Or just spend the whole time talking about random stuff again," Rosy added, laughing. "But that's okay too."

As they packed up their things, Jack glanced at the clock on his wristwatch and realized how late it had gotten. "Do you need a ride home?" he asked. "I've got my pod parked nearby."

Rosy shook her head. "Thanks, but I think I'll walk. It's a nice night, and I kind of want to see more of the city."

"Alright, but be careful. And if you get lost, just call me," Jack said, trying to sound casual, though he couldn't hide the hint of concern in his voice.

"I will," she said, smiling. "See you tomorrow, Jack."

As she turned to leave, Jack watched her for a moment, a small smile on his face. He couldn't quite explain it, but there was something about Rosy that made him feel... lighter. Maybe it was the way she was

BEYOND THE STARS

so passionate about what she did, or maybe it was just the way she made everything seem more interesting. Whatever it was, he was glad they were working together.

The next day, they met up again in the lab, and the pattern continued. They'd work on their project, discussing their findings and bouncing ideas off each other, but inevitably, the conversation would drift to other topics. They talked about their favorite books, their thoughts on the future of space travel, and even the differences between life on Earth and the Moon. Jack found himself looking forward to these sessions more and more, not just because of the project, but because he enjoyed spending time with Rosy.

One evening, as they were wrapping up for the day, Rosy asked, "Do you think people will ever live on planets outside our solar system?"

Jack thought for a moment before answering. "Maybe. I mean, we've done pretty well so far, right? Mars, Venus, the Moon... it's only a matter of time before we start looking further out. But it's going to take a lot of work, and a lot of new ideas."

"Yeah," Rosy said softly. "Maybe someday, we'll find a way to make every planet a little bit like home."

Jack looked at her, seeing the quiet determination in her eyes. "If anyone can figure it out, I bet it'll be you."

She smiled, her cheeks turning a light shade of pink. "And maybe you'll build the robots to help me do it."

Jack laughed. "Sounds like a plan."

As the days went by, their project began to take shape, but more importantly, so did their friendship. They weren't just working together; they were building something—something that felt exciting and new. And as they delved deeper into their research, they found themselves looking forward not just to the results of their project, but to the time they spent together, learning about each other and dreaming about the future.

Chapter 5: First Adventure Beyond Earth

The university halls were buzzing with excitement as news of the upcoming *field trip to Mars* spread among the students. For Jack and Rosy, the announcement felt like the perfect opportunity—not just to further their research on interplanetary ecosystems but to experience firsthand what it was like to be on another planet. Jack had always dreamed of leaving Earth, and now that dream was becoming a reality. When they found out they had both been selected for the trip, they could hardly contain their excitement.

"Can you believe it?" Jack said, practically bouncing with enthusiasm as he walked beside Rosy. "We're actually going to Mars!"

"I know!" Rosy replied, her eyes shining. "I've been off the Moon before, but Mars... it's so different. I've always wanted to see the red plains up close, and now we're going to be right there, in the middle of it all."

The two of them had spent the past week preparing, going over their project notes and planning out what they wanted to focus on during their trip. The field trip was set up to give students a closer look at the *agricultural and atmospheric engineering* taking place on Mars, where scientists were pushing the limits of technology to make the red planet more livable. Jack and Rosy knew it would be the perfect chance to gather data for their project on how different environments were adapted for human habitation.

The day of the trip arrived, and the students gathered at the *Interplanetary Transport Terminal* on the outskirts of the city. The terminal was a massive, sleek structure, with docking bays for spacecraft and bustling crowds of travelers heading to destinations across the solar system. For Jack, the sight was both exhilarating and a bit intimidating. He had never been on a spacecraft before, and the thought of leaving Earth felt surreal.

Rosy nudged him with her elbow, grinning. "Nervous?"

"A little," Jack admitted, glancing up at the massive spacecraft they'd be boarding. It was sleek and streamlined, designed for speed, with a metallic sheen that reflected the sunlight. "But mostly excited. I mean, Mars... who wouldn't be excited?"

Rosy laughed. "Well, you're in for a treat. Trust me, the first time you see another planet up close, it's going to blow your mind."

They boarded the *spacecraft*, finding seats next to each other near one of the large observation windows. As the engines hummed to life and the ship began to ascend, Jack couldn't help but press his face against the glass, watching as the cityscape of Earth grew smaller and smaller below them. Soon, they were above the clouds, and then the sky turned dark, dotted with the faint glow of stars.

The journey was smooth, and within a few hours, they were nearing Mars. Jack's heart raced as the red planet came into view, its surface dotted with craters and vast, rust-colored plains stretching out as far as the eye could see. The spacecraft descended gently, and soon, they were passing over *Mars City*, a sprawling metropolis built under a series of interconnected domes. The domes glowed with a soft, warm light, creating an almost otherworldly effect against the crimson backdrop.

"Wow..." Jack breathed, unable to tear his eyes away from the view. "It's beautiful."

"It really is," Rosy agreed, leaning closer to him so they could both look out the window. "I remember the first time I saw Mars from space. It felt like... like I was looking at a whole new world. And I guess I was."

The spacecraft landed smoothly at *Mars City Central*, and the students disembarked, stepping out into the bustling hub of the city.

BEYOND THE STARS

The air was crisp, cool, and had a slight metallic tang, a reminder that it was being carefully regulated and filtered within the domes. Jack took a deep breath, savoring the sensation of standing on another planet for the first time.

Their first stop was the *Mars Agricultural Research Facility*, where they were given a tour of the massive greenhouses that stretched out under the domes. Rows upon rows of crops—wheat, vegetables, and even some fruits—grew in the red soil, nurtured by artificial light and a carefully controlled atmosphere. Jack was amazed at how green everything was, considering the harsh environment outside the domes.

A guide, a scientist in a white lab coat, led them through the facility, explaining how the crops were genetically engineered to survive in low temperatures and high levels of radiation. "We've had to adapt plants in ways that were never necessary on Earth," she said, her voice carrying a tone of pride. "But thanks to advances in *genetic engineering*, we can grow food here that's not only nutritious but also resilient. We're even working on developing crops that can be planted outside the domes, in the natural Martian soil."

"Is that even possible?" Jack asked, his curiosity piqued.

"It's not easy," the guide admitted. "But we've made some progress. The key is to modify the plants' genes to make them more resistant to the conditions here—low temperatures, low air pressure, and high radiation levels. It's a challenge, but if we succeed, it'll mean that Mars can sustain a much larger population."

As they moved through the facility, Jack and Rosy exchanged excited whispers, jotting down notes and snapping pictures with their wrist devices. They were already coming up with ideas for their project, inspired by everything they were seeing.

After the tour, they were given some free time to explore *Mars City*. Jack and Rosy decided to head to the *Observation Dome*, a large, transparent structure that offered a breathtaking view of the Martian landscape. They stood side by side, looking out at the vast red plains stretching out into the distance. The sky was a pale, dusty pink, and in the distance, they could see the faint outline of *Olympus Mons*, the largest volcano in the solar system.

"Look," Rosy said, pointing. "You can see Earth from here."

Jack squinted, and sure enough, there it was—a tiny blue dot in the sky, barely visible against the expanse of space. Seeing it from this perspective, it looked so small, so fragile. "Wow," he said quietly. "I never thought I'd see Earth from this angle. It's... kind of humbling."

Rosy nodded. "It really makes you realize how connected everything is, doesn't it? Like, we're all just... out here, trying to make it work."

They stood there for a while, just watching the horizon. Jack felt a sense of awe, not just at the view but at the fact that he was sharing this moment with Rosy. It felt like one of those rare, perfect moments where everything seemed to align, and he found himself wishing it wouldn't end.

The rest of their time on Mars was a whirlwind of exploration. They visited the Mars Cultural Center, where they learned about the history of the colonization efforts and the challenges of establishing a sustainable community on the planet. They even sampled some local cuisine, which included dishes made from crops grown in the Martian soil.

"You have to try this," Rosy said, handing Jack a piece of Martian flatbread. "It's made with wheat grown right here, in the domes."

Jack took a bite, surprised at how fresh and flavorful it was. "This is amazing. I didn't think they could grow stuff like this on Mars."

Rosy smiled. "It just shows how far we've come. A few decades ago, the idea of growing food on Mars was just a dream. Now, it's a reality."

By the time the field trip was over, Jack and Rosy had gathered more than enough information for their project. But more importantly, they had shared an experience that brought them closer together. They had seen the ingenuity of human beings, the incredible lengths they

BEYOND THE STARS

had gone to make life possible on a barren planet, and they had done it side by side.

On their last evening, before boarding the spacecraft back to Earth, they returned to the Observation Dome one last time. The sun was setting, casting a warm, reddish glow across the plains. Jack turned to Rosy, feeling a mix of gratitude and something deeper, something he couldn't quite put into words.

"Thanks for coming with me," he said. "I don't think this trip would have been the same without you."

Rosy looked at him, her eyes soft and warm. "I'm glad I came too. I mean, we came here for the project, but... I think I got a lot more out of it than just research."

Jack felt his heart skip a beat. "Yeah. Me too."

They stood there, watching as the last rays of the sun dipped below the horizon, leaving the sky a deep, velvety blue. In that moment, surrounded by the vast, quiet expanse of Mars, Jack felt like anything was possible. And as he glanced at Rosy, he knew that whatever the future held, he wanted her to be a part of it.

Chapter 6: Exploration and Realization

The weeks following their trip to Mars felt like a whirlwind of excitement and discovery for Jack and Rosy. After the success of their field trip, they both realized there was so much more out there to see—so many places they had only read about in textbooks or seen in documentaries. And now, with their interplanetary travel passes, they had the perfect excuse to explore the solar system beyond their university campus.

On a bright Saturday morning, Jack and Rosy found themselves at the Interplanetary Transport Terminal once again, but this time, it wasn't for a university project. They had decided to make the most of their weekends, using their passes to visit different planets and moons whenever they could. Their first destination after Mars was Venus.

"I've always been curious about those floating cities," Rosy said as they boarded the spacecraft bound for Venus. "I mean, how do they even manage to stay up there, suspended in the clouds?"

Jack grinned, buckling his seatbelt. "We're about to find out. I heard they use these massive blimp-like structures that keep the cities buoyant in the upper atmosphere. The air pressure there is close to Earth's, so it's the only place humans can really live on Venus."

Rosy's eyes lit up. "I can't wait to see it. Just imagine—cities floating in a sea of clouds... it sounds like something out of a dream."

As the spacecraft took off, Jack found himself looking forward not just to the destination but to the journey itself. Sitting beside Rosy, he felt a sense of anticipation, knowing that they were about to embark on yet another adventure together. The flight to Venus was smooth, and soon they were descending through the thick, yellowish clouds, the view outside the windows shifting from the dark expanse of space to the swirling, misty atmosphere of Venus.

The Venusian cloud cities were unlike anything Jack had ever seen. Suspended high above the planet's boiling, inhospitable surface, the cities were held aloft by massive, helium-filled structures that looked like giant balloons. Below them, the clouds stretched out endlessly, a vast, swirling sea of vapor. As the spacecraft approached the docking bay, Jack and Rosy could see sleek, white buildings with domed roofs and tall spires, gleaming in the soft, golden light that filtered through the clouds.

They stepped out into the main promenade of Helios City, one of the largest cloud cities on Venus. The air was warm and slightly humid, but comfortable, and there was a gentle, almost dreamlike quality to the place. People strolled along walkways lined with lush, green plants, and small drones buzzed overhead, delivering packages and performing maintenance.

"It's like walking in a cloud," Rosy said, looking around with wide-eyed wonder. "I never imagined it would be so... peaceful."

"Yeah," Jack agreed, taking in the serene atmosphere. "It's hard to believe that just a few kilometers below us, it's a raging inferno of acid storms and crushing pressure."

They spent the day exploring Helios City, learning about the innovative technology that allowed the city to float, as well as the various methods used to harvest water and energy from the atmosphere. Jack was particularly fascinated by the massive turbines that generated electricity from the powerful winds, while Rosy was more interested in the hydroponic gardens that provided food for the city's inhabitants.

After their tour, they found a café with a stunning view of the clouds, and they sat by the window, sipping drinks made from locally-grown fruits. "So," Jack said, glancing at Rosy, "where to next? We've got the whole solar system to choose from."

Rosy smiled, twirling her straw thoughtfully. "I've always wanted to see Europa. I mean, there's a whole ocean under the ice there, and who knows what could be swimming around down there? It just seems... mysterious."

"Europa it is, then," Jack said, nodding. "I've heard there are observation stations on the surface where you can actually see them drilling through the ice to study the ocean below. We should definitely check that out."

As they planned their next trip, Jack realized how easy it was to talk to Rosy—how natural it felt to share his thoughts and ideas with her. It was as if, without even realizing it, they had become partners, not just in their university projects but in this new journey of exploration.

Over the following weekends, Jack and Rosy visited Europa, Saturn, and even a leisure station orbiting Titan. Each trip was a new adventure, with its own set of surprises. On Europa, they marveled at the vast, icy plains, the surface glistening under the distant sunlight. They stood at the edge of a massive drilling site, watching as scientists extracted samples from the subsurface ocean, hoping to find signs of microbial life.

"I wonder if there's anything down there," Jack mused, staring at the drilling machinery. "I mean, actual, living organisms. Imagine if we're not alone, even in our own solar system."

Rosy leaned against the railing, her breath visible in the cold air. "It would change everything, wouldn't it? The way we see ourselves, the way we think about life. I think that's why I love exploring—because there's always the possibility of discovering something new, something that changes everything."

Jack looked at her, feeling a warm sense of admiration. "You're always thinking ahead, aren't you? I like that about you."

Rosy blushed slightly but didn't look away. "And you're always so curious. It's like... you see the world in a way that makes me want to see more of it, too."

Their conversation was interrupted by the sound of a drill hitting something beneath the ice, sending a shiver through the ground. They both jumped, then laughed at their shared surprise. It was moments like these—unexpected, spontaneous, and full of wonder—that seemed to bring them closer together.

Their trips continued, each one adding new layers to their friendship. On Saturn's leisure station, they spent an afternoon lounging in a café that had a panoramic view of the planet's iconic rings. The rings shimmered in the sunlight, casting a soft, ethereal glow that filled the room.

"Can you imagine living here?" Rosy asked, sipping her drink. "Waking up every day to a view like this?"

Jack glanced at the rings, then back at Rosy. "It would be amazing," he said, though he knew that no view, no matter how beautiful, could compare to the feeling of being here with her. "But I think it would be even better with the right company."

Rosy looked at him, and for a moment, there was a quiet, unspoken understanding between them. It wasn't just about the places they visited or the things they saw—it was about experiencing it all together. Jack felt his heart skip a beat, realizing just how much he enjoyed being with Rosy, how much he wanted to share not just these adventures but everything with her.

On their final evening at the Saturn station, they found a spot on the observation deck, sitting side by side as the sun dipped behind the planet's rings, casting long shadows across the sky. The stars began to emerge, one by one, until the whole expanse of space was twinkling above them.

"It's beautiful," Rosy said softly, her voice barely more than a whisper. "I wish we could just... stay here, like this, forever."

BEYOND THE STARS

Jack turned to her, feeling a strange mix of emotions—excitement, nervousness, and a warmth that he couldn't quite explain. "Rosy, I—"

She looked at him, her eyes reflecting the starlight. "Jack?"

"I just... I'm glad we're doing this," he said, fumbling for the right words. "I'm glad it's you I'm exploring all of this with."

Rosy smiled, and in that moment, it was as if the whole universe had faded away, leaving just the two of them. "Me too, Jack. I wouldn't want to be anywhere else."

As they sat there, watching the rings of Saturn glisten in the fading light, Jack felt a sense of peace, a certainty that he hadn't felt in a long time. They were no longer just friends, no longer just classmates. They were partners—explorers in a vast, endless universe, bound together by a connection that was growing stronger with each passing day.

And as they gazed out into the infinite, starry sky, Jack realized that their journey was only just beginning.

Chapter 7: A Journey to the Moon

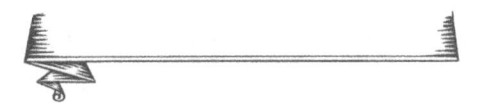

The silver gleam of the Lunar Transit Station felt as futuristic as it was, humming with quiet energy. Jack and Rosy looked around, feeling the soft thrumming of engines beneath their feet as they walked through the embarkation area. Lunar travel had become so streamlined that it almost felt like boarding a city tram. Jack was buzzing with excitement, but it was Rosy who held a palpable sense of curiosity. Her eyes sparkled as she adjusted her travel pack, gazing out the port windows that framed a perfect view of Earth from their launch station.

"So, ready for your next lunar adventure?" Jack asked with a grin, nudging Rosy as they took their seats.

"I can't believe it's happening," she replied, brushing a stray lock of hair behind her ear. "There's so much groundbreaking research happening there, especially in bioengineering. I've been reading up on the facility—rumor has it they're on the verge of some huge breakthroughs that could even make Venus habitable."

Jack chuckled. "Good thing we're visiting then, huh? Plus, I'd say having a real expert like you along makes the trip twice as exciting."

As the engines whirred and the pressure stabilized, they felt the slight push as the transit shuttle eased out of Earth's atmosphere. Rosy gave Jack a quick, excited smile. For both of them, this was a kind of dream trip.

The arrival on the Moon was surreal. When they disembarked, the grand white architecture of the Lunar Scientific Research Center sprawled across the barren landscape like a shining jewel. Jack couldn't help but feel a sense of awe; everything looked sterile, futuristic, and massive. Scientists in sleek lab coats and automated carts buzzed around as if it were the most normal place in the universe.

The guide greeted them with a nod and led them into the main lobby. "Welcome to the Lunar Scientific Research Center, where we're pushing the boundaries of human habitation in space," she began. "Over here, we have the genetic labs working on atmospheric adaptation plants, and in the adjoining wings, you'll find departments dedicated to mineral research, biotechnological enhancement, and planetary survival strategies."

As they continued the tour, Rosy's eyes lit up. She was completely absorbed, asking questions at each exhibit they passed, her curiosity driving them forward. Jack smiled, watching her enthusiasm with amusement.

"Hey, check this out," she whispered to Jack, nudging him towards an area filled with towering specimens of modified flora, plants that glowed with a faint greenish hue. "This species can photosynthesize using wavelengths more suited to low-light environments, which is perfect for Mars or the Moon."

Jack examined the plants with interest, tracing a finger along the transparent shield protecting the samples. "Guess we might be seeing forests on Mars sooner than we thought, huh?"

"Maybe sooner than you think," Rosy replied with a smile.

The guide led them deeper into the facility, finally bringing them to a heavily secured wing. "Now, I should mention," she said with a slight frown, "beyond this point is restricted to personnel only. Classified experiments and sensitive equipment. However, I hope you enjoyed seeing our more public breakthroughs."

BEYOND THE STARS

As the guide left, Rosy nudged Jack, lowering her voice. "Is it just me, or does it feel like there's more going on here than they're letting on?"

Jack glanced around, catching sight of a barely noticeable door tucked away in a corner, marked only by a small metal plaque with no label. The door was cracked open, a warm light seeping through.

"Now that you mention it..." Jack trailed off, drawn toward the door. Rosy raised an eyebrow, her face lit with curiosity.

"Jack, are you really thinking of snooping?" she whispered, though her expression betrayed her own intrigue.

"It's just a peek," Jack replied with a grin, "and besides, I doubt they'd put this much effort into security if there was nothing worth seeing." He took a step toward the door, gesturing for Rosy to follow. They both exchanged a mischievous look before slipping inside.

✕

Inside, the atmosphere changed completely. The room was dimly lit, with stacks of crates lining the walls, and the air held a faint whiff of something metallic and pungent. Jack's heart pounded as they hid behind a crate, staying out of sight.

At the far end of the room, several figures stood in a huddle, their conversation hushed. They were dressed differently than the scientists they'd seen outside, wearing thick jackets with hoods up, casting shadows over their faces. Jack noticed a man with a powerful build, standing slightly apart from the others. His voice cut through the quiet like a blade.

"...just remember, if we don't move the next shipment to the Martian outposts soon, we'll lose our edge in the sector. These deliveries are the only way we keep things afloat," the man said in a low, commanding tone.

"Robusco, you don't have to remind us. But we need to bypass the transport authority. They're scanning shipments now," replied another figure.

"Then we'll pay them off," Robusco said with a shrug, pulling a small data chip from his pocket and handing it to the nearest figure. "This will grant access to the holding areas on Mars without triggering a single alarm. Make sure no one suspects anything."

Jack's eyes widened as he heard the name. Robusco—he'd heard it whispered before, a name tied to underground dealings throughout the solar system.

"Jack, this sounds bad," Rosy murmured, gripping his arm tightly.

"I know," he replied, his voice barely above a whisper. They crouched even lower, hardly daring to breathe as the group continued their exchange.

Another figure spoke up, holding a small holo-display showing a layout of some kind of ship. "With this tech, we could bypass any security system on the lunar bases as well. And if we secure this planet, Earth is just a jump away."

Robusco nodded approvingly. "Good. Make sure everything is ready by next cycle. I want this done before anyone catches on."

Jack swallowed hard. The realization of what they were witnessing hit him like a wave: this wasn't just a small operation; it was a coordinated smuggling network reaching across planets, possibly even back to Earth. Just then, one of the figures turned slightly, eyes sweeping the room, and Jack felt his heart skip a beat. He pulled Rosy back, holding his breath as they waited for the figure's attention to shift away again.

"Let's get out of here," Jack mouthed, his expression tense.

Rosy nodded, and together, they backed out of the room as quietly as they could, slipping into the corridor just as the door clicked shut behind them. They exchanged a look, faces flushed with adrenaline.

"We have to tell someone," Jack said, his voice shaking slightly.

Rosy's expression was troubled. "But who? This is way bigger than just a simple campus issue. What if Robusco has connections even here?"

Jack ran a hand through his hair, the weight of the situation settling in. "I don't know. But we can't just let this go. If they're transporting tech that dangerous—"

Rosy put a hand on his arm. "Let's get back to our lodgings and think this through. We need to plan carefully. If Robusco's operation is as big as it seems, we have to be smart about this."

They glanced over their shoulders, still half-expecting someone to appear out of nowhere, before making their way through the sterile halls of the research center. As they walked back toward the transit station, Jack felt a new weight in his chest. What started as a casual trip to the Moon had become a life-changing moment, and he knew that whatever happened next, he and Rosy were already in much deeper than they had anticipated.

Chapter 8: Uncovering the Scheme

Jack and Rosy sat across from each other in their modest lodging on the Moon, both still shaken from their encounter with Robusco's group. The walls around them seemed to close in with the weight of what they had stumbled upon, making the low hum of the air systems feel louder than usual. Jack ran his fingers through his hair, a look of concentration on his face, while Rosy gazed out the small window, staring at the stars just beyond the dome.

"What do we do now?" Jack finally broke the silence, his voice barely above a whisper.

Rosy turned back to him, her eyes filled with a mixture of fear and determination. "We can't just sit on this information, Jack. But if we go straight to the authorities, who's to say Robusco doesn't have connections there too? We don't know how deep this thing runs."

Jack sighed, leaning back in his seat. "I know, but...if they're smuggling tech that dangerous, it could be catastrophic. Who knows what kind of damage they could do if it falls into the wrong hands?"

Rosy bit her lip, thinking. "What if we gather more information first? Figure out exactly what's going on and who's involved. That way, if we go to someone, we have more than just suspicions."

Jack looked at her, considering. "But what if we get caught? We don't exactly have experience with this whole 'secret investigation' thing, Rosy."

A faint smile tugged at the corner of Rosy's mouth. "No, but we do have each other. And we're both pretty good at asking questions." She leaned forward, her expression serious. "Let's go back to the research center. We'll just be two curious students, here to study."

The next morning, they returned to the research center with a careful sense of purpose, masking their apprehension with feigned enthusiasm for their "studies." The facility felt even more imposing now, the sterile hallways and futuristic labs looming with a strange, new sense of menace. They made their way to one of the more populated areas, hoping to hear something that might give them a lead without drawing too much attention.

As they walked, Rosy glanced over at Jack. "We should start by casually asking around. Maybe mention Robusco's name and see if anyone reacts."

Jack nodded. "Just don't be too direct. The last thing we need is someone reporting us to...well, whoever's working with him here."

Their first stop was a lounge area where employees gathered to recharge. Jack struck up a conversation with a young researcher who was idly scrolling through data on a holo-screen.

"So, what brings you here?" the researcher asked casually, adjusting his visor. "Not many students get clearance for the Lunar Center."

"Oh, we're part of an interplanetary ecosystems project back on Earth," Jack replied smoothly. "It's our first time here, and honestly, we're just trying to wrap our heads around everything. It's incredible how much happens up here."

The researcher nodded, a proud smile creeping onto his face. "Yeah, the research here's top-notch. We're doing things that'll change humanity forever. But...not everyone's here for the science, if you know what I mean."

Rosy raised her eyebrows, feigning innocence. "Really? I thought only researchers and scientists worked here."

BEYOND THE STARS

"Well, for the most part, yeah," the researcher said, lowering his voice slightly. "But...there are rumors, you know? People talk. Some say that there's an underground network, moving things across the solar system that probably shouldn't be moved."

Jack and Rosy exchanged a look.

"What kind of...things?" Rosy asked, trying to sound casual.

The researcher shrugged, his eyes darting around the lounge. "No one really knows for sure. But I've heard people mention names. Like there's this one guy...Robusco, I think? He's said to have connections everywhere—Mars, Europa, even the outer colonies. People say he's untouchable."

"Interesting," Jack murmured, trying to keep his face neutral. "Wonder what it's like to operate on that level."

"Careful," the researcher said with a wry smile, leaning back in his seat. "People who get curious about him usually find themselves in...let's just say, 'unfavorable' situations."

Over the next few days, Jack and Rosy continued to visit the center, carefully piecing together snippets of conversation and trying to piece together the bigger picture. They discovered hints of an extensive network, stretching across the solar system. Robusco's operation seemed to revolve around transporting unauthorized tech and resources to places where they could be exploited. The more they learned, the clearer it became that this wasn't just a minor smuggling ring—it was a full-scale operation with contacts on nearly every inhabited planet.

One evening, as they were wrapping up their "study session" in one of the research center's quieter sections, they were interrupted by a low voice behind them.

"You two have been asking a lot of questions."

Jack and Rosy spun around to see a tall, shadowy figure standing in the doorway, his arms crossed. His face was half-hidden in the dim light, but his voice carried a chilling calmness that made the hairs on Jack's arms stand up.

"Curiosity can be dangerous up here," the man continued, his gaze fixed on them. "People who stick their noses where they don't belong usually don't stick around for long."

Rosy took a step back, her face pale. "W-we were just...just studying. We're students, you know? Here for the research."

The man smirked. "I've heard that line before. Let me give you some advice—stop digging. You don't want to be part of this, trust me." His voice dropped to a menacing whisper. "Not if you value your lives."

With that, he turned and walked out, leaving them frozen in shock.

Back in their lodging that night, Jack and Rosy were too shaken to sleep. They sat across from each other, the words of the mysterious stranger echoing in their minds.

"Do you think he was serious?" Rosy whispered, her face etched with worry.

Jack nodded slowly. "This isn't just a harmless operation, Rosy. They're willing to threaten people just for asking questions. But that makes me think...maybe we're onto something bigger than we thought."

Rosy looked at him, her eyes filled with a mixture of fear and determination. "Then what do we do?"

"We keep digging," Jack said, his voice steady. "But we have to be smarter about it. If Robusco and his people know we're onto them, we need to make sure they can't find us, or at least not easily."

Rosy nodded, her expression resolute. "Then we stay low, but we keep going. If we don't, who will?"

BEYOND THE STARS

Jack reached out, giving her hand a reassuring squeeze. "We're in this together, Rosy. Whatever happens, we'll face it head-on."

As the night wore on, they talked in whispers, carefully planning their next moves. They knew the risks, but the thought of turning back felt impossible now. They had seen too much, learned too much. And they both knew they couldn't stand by and let something so dangerous unfold unchecked.

When they finally drifted off to sleep, it was with a sense of purpose—and a shadow of fear that loomed over them, a reminder of the dark forces they were up against.

Chapter 9: The Chase Begins

Under the artificial twilight of the lunar dome, Jack and Rosy moved with cautious purpose, blending into the steady flow of people navigating the bustling lunar docking station. The vast expanse of the station stretched out before them, dotted with clusters of cargo and crisscrossed by pathways leading to various gates. They had tracked Robusco here, hoping for a face-to-face encounter that might grant them a chance to play the role of innocent students, fishing for answers.

"Do you see him?" Jack whispered, scanning the docks from behind a metal column.

Rosy narrowed her eyes and nodded. "Over there, by the unmarked ship," she replied, gesturing subtly toward a distant bay where Robusco and his team were gathered, loading equipment into an angular, unregistered spacecraft. The ship's dull metal hull caught only the faintest glint of the docking bay's lights, camouflaging it against the metallic grays of the station. Robusco's presence radiated a powerful authority, his stance relaxed but guarded, every movement of his calculated as he watched his crew load the cargo.

Jack and Rosy huddled behind a row of stacked crates, their nerves taut. "All right," Jack whispered. "If we just act like clueless students, maybe he won't see us as a threat."

Rosy swallowed hard. "And if he does?"

Jack squeezed her hand. "Then we run." His tone was calm, but Rosy could feel the tension in his grip.

They moved quietly, ducking behind crates and sneaking closer, hoping to catch a glimpse of what was being loaded onto the ship. Between the crates, Jack caught sight of a box labeled Terraforming Equipment – High Grade. He frowned and exchanged a look with Rosy, who nodded grimly. This wasn't just minor equipment; these were critical resources used for large-scale planetary adaptation. Whatever Robusco was involved in, it wasn't just petty smuggling—it was something that could impact entire ecosystems.

As they leaned in to listen, they heard Robusco's gravelly voice drift across the bay.

"...all set, then?" he asked, directing his question to a man standing beside him—a tall, imposing figure in a dark uniform.

"Yes, sir," the man replied. "We'll have everything out and ready for the rendezvous with the Mars team. They'll need the equipment in a few weeks if they want to stay on schedule."

"Good," Robusco said, his tone matter-of-fact. "Make sure it's secure. If anyone notices this shipment is missing, we're all in deep."

The lieutenant nodded. "Don't worry. This isn't our first operation. Everything's been paid off, and security's already been cleared. No one will suspect a thing."

Jack's heart pounded as he processed their words. They were planning to divert an entire shipment of terraforming equipment? The implications were staggering. Without that equipment, Mars' fragile colonies would be at risk. Lives could be at stake.

Rosy leaned close, her voice barely above a whisper. "We have to stop this, Jack. Mars won't survive without that equipment."

Jack clenched his jaw, nodding. "But how?"

Just as they were trying to figure out their next move, a sharp clanging sound echoed nearby. Both of them froze, realizing they'd accidentally knocked a small tool off a nearby crate. The noise drew the attention of one of the guards, who turned, eyes narrowing in their direction.

BEYOND THE STARS

"Who's there?" the guard called out, his hand moving to his holster. Panic flashed across Rosy's face. "Jack, we need to go—now."

They took off, darting between stacks of crates as shouts rang out behind them. Heavy footsteps pounded as the guards gave chase, their voices barking commands as they closed in.

"Split up," Jack hissed, pulling Rosy to the side of a narrow passage. "We'll meet back at the transport pods!"

Rosy nodded, her eyes wide with fear but resolute. "Stay safe, Jack." She sprinted in the opposite direction, weaving between crates and boxes, her footsteps light and quick.

Jack dashed down another corridor, his heart racing as he heard the guards closing in behind him. The maze of crates felt both like a sanctuary and a trap, each turn offering a new hiding spot but also more chances to be cornered. He dove behind a stack of crates, pressing himself flat against the cold metal as he heard footsteps thunder past, the guards cursing as they scanned the area.

Holding his breath, Jack waited until the footsteps faded before sneaking around a side exit. He bolted across the docking bay floor, weaving through workers and travelers who glanced at him in surprise. He had no time to explain, his mind focused solely on escaping and finding Rosy.

Meanwhile, Rosy had managed to lose her pursuers by slipping into a storage area. She crouched behind a pallet, catching her breath as she listened to the chaos echoing through the docking bay. She knew Jack was out there somewhere, just as determined as she was to make it out. She couldn't bear the thought of being caught alone—especially not after all they'd risked together.

After what felt like an eternity, she finally spotted him near the entrance to the transport pods. Relief washed over her as she saw his familiar figure scanning the crowd, looking for her. She raised a hand, waving urgently.

"Jack!" she called, running up to him.

"Are you okay?" he asked, his eyes scanning her face for any signs of injury.

"Yeah, I think so. But we need to go. They'll still be looking for us."

They scrambled into one of the transport pods, hitting the controls as the doors slid shut behind them. The pod hummed to life, pulling away from the docking station as they finally allowed themselves to exhale. The glow of the Moon's surface passed by outside the window as they sped away, leaving the chaos behind them.

After a few moments of silence, Jack spoke, his voice quiet but resolute. "This is bigger than we thought, Rosy. Robusco's operation—it's dangerous. And it's only a matter of time before they realize we're onto them."

Rosy nodded, a fierce determination in her eyes. "But we can't stop now. Not after what we saw. People are depending on that equipment, Jack. We have to figure out a way to stop him before it's too late."

Jack reached out, giving her hand a reassuring squeeze. "Then we keep going. We find out everything we can, but we have to be smarter about it. No more slip-ups."

They lapsed into silence, the weight of their decision settling heavily between them. They were no longer just students on a field trip. In that chase, they had crossed a line—a line that bound them to a mission they could no longer walk away from.

As the transport pod sped through the lunar night, Jack and Rosy shared a solemn understanding. They were now fugitives in a world where secrets were currency, where alliances were hidden, and where every move they made would have to be carefully calculated.

Their journey had become more than just an adventure. It was now a battle between what was right and what was safe—and they both knew, deep down, that they'd chosen a path that was far from safe.

Chapter 10: Digging Deeper

Jack had barely caught his breath since returning to Earth. The close call with Robusco's crew on the Moon had him rattled, yet it hadn't extinguished his desire to dig deeper. In fact, the danger only fueled his resolve. Rosy shared his sentiment; the grim understanding that Robusco's operation could jeopardize the safety of innocent people had left her restless. They'd seen enough to know this wasn't just smuggling—this was something dark, far-reaching, and dangerous.

Initial Research

It was late in the afternoon, and the university library was nearly empty. Sunlight streamed through the high, dome-shaped glass ceilings, casting geometric patterns across the polished floors. Jack was seated at a sleek computer console, his eyes focused on lines of archived articles, legal records, and security logs. Rosy was beside him, sorting through any related data she could find on her tablet.

"Here's something interesting," Rosy whispered, nudging Jack. "There's a company listed under his name called Tech Sapiens. It's supposed to be a 'consultancy' for interplanetary research, but no one really knows what it does. Strange, right?"

Jack leaned in, his interest piqued. "And if he's fronting an operation under that cover... we might be onto something. What else can we find?"

They combed through more public records, gradually forming a vague trail that linked Robusco to various corporations and shadowy entities across Mars, Venus, and even the outer asteroid belts. It was a well-woven web, crafted to keep any curious minds at bay, but they could see enough threads to understand its scale.

Rosy clicked into a suspicious-looking news article. "Listen to this: 'Authorities recently confiscated unauthorized biotech mods near Mars Station 3.' That's exactly what we saw on the Moon—the biotech equipment."

Jack's eyes widened. "So he's been smuggling this stuff across the entire solar system."

Rosy's face grew concerned. "But what's the end goal? These mods, they're dangerous. They're not just gadgets; they could destabilize ecosystems, maybe even worse..."

Jack nodded. "Let's not get ahead of ourselves. Right now, we need more concrete proof."

Gathering Evidence

That evening, Jack and Rosy decided it was time to push the limits. They needed something Robusco couldn't refute, something that directly tied him to smuggling and his potential buyers.

In the quiet of Rosy's apartment, Jack set up his portable console on the dining table, linking into a low-security channel through a VPN. He knew there was a risk, but it was one they had to take. Rosy watched over his shoulder as he carefully bypassed the security layers on the lunar research center's server, their gateway to tracking Robusco's operations.

"Careful," Rosy warned as she poured over some notes on her tablet, "Remember, we're looking for files related to hazardous shipments."

Jack nodded, his fingers moving swiftly over the console's interface. "Trust me, I'm doing my best to stay low-profile."

After several tense minutes, he finally found an encrypted folder with a suspicious title: "Tech Logistics 2702." Jack's heart pounded as he began decrypting the files. The screen filled with logs, receipts, and manifests—all tied to strange shipments, labeled only with codes.

"Look here," he whispered, scrolling down. "Delivery records to Mars, Venus... even the asteroid belt. And these codes—'H-13-BT'? Rosy, I think these stand for hazardous bio-tech mods."

Her face grew grim as she scanned through the files. "These mods aren't just experimental; they're dangerous enough to be blacklisted from most planets. If he's been distributing them, who knows what kind of damage he could cause?"

Jack paused, and a sudden realization hit him. "We're dealing with something that could impact thousands. We have to get this information to someone who can help."

Facing Hurdles

As the files finished decrypting, Rosy's screen suddenly flashed a warning: SECURITY BREACH DETECTED. ACCESS TERMINATED. The warning message loomed large, its crimson font filling her entire screen.

"What just happened?" she gasped, clutching her laptop tightly.

Jack's face blanched. "It means they know. Robusco's network is aware we accessed their data."

Panic flashed across her eyes, but she steadied herself. "Do you think they tracked us?"

Jack shook his head, though he wasn't entirely sure. "We should be safe for now. But we can't stay idle anymore. We need to keep this investigation discreet. Robusco likely has connections even on Earth."

Rosy shut her laptop, still shaken. "Jack, do you realize what this means? We could be targets now, just for looking. Robusco's reach could extend farther than we thought."

Jack met her gaze, his expression determined. "We have to keep going, Rosy. If we give up now, we're letting him go unchecked, and too many people could get hurt."

She managed a small nod. "All right, but we need to be smart about it. No more risky hacks or direct traces."

They decided to switch tactics. Over the next few days, they accessed only public information, sifting through news sites and forums, leaving no trace of their activity. Jack even went as far as using different IP addresses and public servers to minimize any tracking.

An Ominous Warning

One evening, after several hours spent on a public server, Rosy stretched her arms and leaned back, exhausted. She glanced over at Jack. "You know, I can't shake the feeling that someone's watching us."

Jack turned to her, eyebrows raised. "I've felt the same way since that breach warning. But no one's approached us yet."

Just as he said it, a notification popped up on his watch: Unknown number. Voice message received.

They exchanged a worried glance. Jack hit play, and a gravelly voice echoed from his watch speaker. "Back off, or you'll regret it. Robusco doesn't like snoops."

Jack's stomach dropped. Rosy's face went pale.

"How did they get your number?" she whispered.

Jack shook his head, stunned. "They're closer than we thought. And if they know this much, we have to assume they'll be watching our every move."

They sat in tense silence, the gravity of the situation setting in. It was no longer a theoretical risk; they were now on Robusco's radar.

But instead of retreating, the warning only solidified their resolve. Jack's gaze steeled as he looked at Rosy. "We'll be careful, but we're not stopping."

Rosy smiled faintly, matching his determination. "Good. Because someone has to stop him, and we're already too deep to turn back now."

With renewed focus, they formulated a plan to move forward, no longer just students but investigators, stepping into a battle that would determine the fate of countless lives across the solar system. They knew the stakes, and no matter the danger, they were ready.

Chapter 11: Into Dangerous Waters

Jack and Rosy were no strangers to the late-night hum of the university's labs, but this time, their surroundings felt heavier, as though an invisible force was bearing down on them. The revelation about Robusco's operations had shaken them both. What had started as a curiosity-driven investigation had turned into something more sinister and dangerous.

Expanding the Investigation

They had questions. Too many, in fact, to ignore. But they knew they needed more minds to get to the bottom of Robusco's smuggling operation—especially those with insights into bioengineering and robotics. So, they decided to reach out to people they could trust.

In a small office down the hall from their lab, Professor Alan Moretti was sitting, arms folded, listening intently to Jack and Rosy's story. Professor Moretti, a robotics expert and mentor to Jack, was one of the few people who had taken his interest in interplanetary tech seriously from the start. His steady gaze shifted between Jack and Rosy as they explained Robusco's scheme, the risky encounter at the lunar station, and the encrypted files they had managed to access.

"What you're telling me," Professor Moretti said slowly, "is that you believe Robusco has been moving dangerous technology that could potentially affect planetary ecosystems?"

Rosy nodded, her expression solemn. "It's not just about smuggling; we think he's distributing biotech modifications, ones that were banned from major colonies because of their potential to destabilize entire habitats. Professor, if someone used this tech maliciously, the effects could be catastrophic."

Moretti leaned back, his face grim. "I've heard whispers about people like Robusco, opportunists who operate on the fringes of the law, but I never thought his operations would be this... extensive." He paused, studying them with narrowed eyes. "Jack, Rosy, do you understand the kind of people you're dealing with here? Robusco isn't just some rogue trader. If he's involved in the kinds of activities you're describing, you're putting yourselves in serious danger."

Jack swallowed, sensing the gravity of Moretti's words. "We know, Professor. But if we don't do something, who will? No one else knows what he's doing, or the scale of it. And what about the impact this could have on the colonies?"

Professor Moretti sighed. "All right, I'll help in whatever way I can. But please, be careful. There are people who will go to great lengths to protect their interests—especially those with reach across multiple planets." He glanced at Rosy. "And you... you said there were modifications that could impact oxygen supplies on colonies?"

Rosy nodded, her gaze serious. "Yes, Professor. Some of these mods can disrupt systems on remote outposts, like synthetic photosynthesis modules. If someone altered these modules, it could trigger a domino effect, impacting oxygen production. On a closed ecosystem like a lunar base or Martian outpost, that could be deadly."

The professor's face went pale as he absorbed the implications. "If Robusco is involved in something that dangerous, this goes beyond just smuggling. It's reckless and potentially catastrophic." He took a deep breath. "Look, I can put you in touch with Dr. Elena Weiss in the bioengineering department. She's been researching stable biosystems for off-world environments. She might know something about these modifications you're describing."

BEYOND THE STARS

Rosy and Jack exchanged a relieved glance. Moretti's advice could open doors for them in understanding the complexities of Robusco's network.

"Thank you, Professor," Jack said quietly. "We'll reach out to Dr. Weiss. And we'll be careful."

Moretti nodded, his expression still troubled. "Just remember, tread lightly. If Robusco has eyes on the university, it won't take him long to realize you're asking questions."

A Risky Meeting

After several days of cautious investigation, Jack managed to arrange a meeting with an associate who, according to the rumors, had once been part of Robusco's inner circle. The contact was wary at first but agreed to meet at a secluded location on the lunar station.

They arrived at the rendezvous point—a quiet, dimly lit cargo bay that had been closed for maintenance. They waited, scanning their surroundings for any sign of movement. Minutes later, a figure emerged from the shadows, his face half-hidden beneath the hood of his coat.

"You Jack?" the man asked in a low voice, his gaze darting around the room.

Jack nodded, doing his best to appear calm. "Thanks for agreeing to meet."

The man looked at Rosy, then back at Jack. "I'm here because I owed a favor, but this is dangerous business you're sticking your nose into. Robusco doesn't take kindly to people poking around."

Jack took a steadying breath. "That's exactly why we need information. Robusco's using dangerous tech mods, ones that could harm the colonies. We need to know more about his network—who's involved, what he's moving, and why."

The man let out a dry laugh. "Kid, you're in over your head if you think Robusco's just a small-time player. His network stretches far beyond the Moon. He's got people on Mars, Venus, and even out in the asteroid belt. Some of his clients are high-level too—corporate types, officials willing to look the other way for the right price."

Rosy's eyes widened. "So, there's no way to stop him?"

The associate shook his head. "There's always a way, but it won't be easy. Robusco's got eyes and ears everywhere. His reach is deep, and he has access to resources you can't even imagine. The authorities have tried to shut him down before, but he's slippery. Too many connections."

Jack clenched his fists, feeling a mix of frustration and resolve. "Do you know what he's planning? Or who he's selling to?"

The associate hesitated, his gaze hardening. "He's working with some powerful players—people who want access to illegal biotech and advanced mods. I heard a rumor that he's been stockpiling terraforming tech—stuff that could wreak havoc if used improperly. Word is, he's selling it to the highest bidder. People who want control over the colonies' resources. If you interfere, you're putting yourselves directly in his line of fire."

The warning hung heavy in the air. Jack glanced at Rosy, whose expression mirrored his own determination.

"What if we can get proof?" Jack asked, his voice steady. "If we can expose him, would that be enough to stop him?"

The man looked at Jack with a weary expression. "Maybe. But you'd need solid evidence, and getting that won't be easy. If he finds out you're close... well, let's just say you'd better watch your back."

With that, the associate turned and disappeared into the shadows, leaving them alone in the cold, dim cargo bay.

Growing Tension

As they made their way back to their quarters, the silence between Jack and Rosy was thick with unspoken thoughts. They had confirmation now—Robusco's network was far more expansive than they had anticipated. He wasn't just a smuggler; he was a power player, dealing in illegal technology that could destabilize the entire solar system.

As they reached their quarters, Rosy spoke, her voice low. "Jack, are we really ready for this? We're no longer just students working on a project. This is... this is real."

Jack nodded, his jaw tight. "I know. But if we walk away now, we'll never forgive ourselves. People's lives are at stake, Rosy. Robusco's got too much power, and someone has to stop him."

Rosy glanced over her shoulder, a chill running down her spine. "Did you... did you feel that?"

Jack followed her gaze but saw nothing unusual. "What?"

"It just felt like... like we were being watched," Rosy whispered.

Jack tensed, his eyes scanning their surroundings. The thought sent a shiver down his spine. Could Robusco already be aware of their movements?

They hurried inside, locking the door behind them. Jack placed his watch on the table, setting it to silent mode. The paranoia had crept into his thoughts as well; every glance, every sound, now felt suspicious.

That night, they worked in silence, each of them feeling the weight of the investigation pressing down on them. They couldn't deny the risks—they were now caught in a web that reached beyond anything they had ever imagined.

As the hours ticked by, Rosy looked up from her console, her voice soft but resolute. "No matter what happens, we stick together. We'll find a way to stop him."

Jack met her gaze, his determination mirroring hers. "Agreed. We're in this together, no matter what. And we're not giving up until Robusco's operation is exposed."

Their resolve strengthened, they continued their work, knowing the road ahead was fraught with danger. But for the first time, they felt as though they had a purpose, a mission that went beyond academic goals. They were no longer just students—they were fighters, standing against a force that threatened the safety of the entire solar system. And no matter how daunting it seemed, they were ready to face it together.

Chapter 12: The Revelation

Jack sat in the dim glow of his desk lamp, fingers tapping the console as he sorted through lines of data that Rosy had helped decrypt. The files were patchy and hard to make sense of, but piece by piece, they were uncovering the full extent of Robusco's operation. Jack glanced at Rosy, who was seated across from him, deeply focused, her brow creased as she scanned through data logs. For weeks now, they had lived and breathed this investigation, each step taking them closer to something enormous and terrifying.

"Look at this," Jack said quietly, pulling up a particularly troubling document. "It's a list of tech that's been smuggled in over the last month alone. Half of these items are on the restricted list—illegal modifications, bioengineered viruses, planetary regulators. All things that could be catastrophic in the wrong hands."

Rosy leaned over, her eyes narrowing as she read the list. "Planetary regulators? Those are supposed to be used for emergencies only, to stabilize ecosystems in case of system failures on colonies. They're closely monitored tech. How is he getting his hands on them?"

Jack ran a hand through his hair, shaking his head. "It's bigger than we thought. Robusco isn't just selling illegal mods; he's gathering high-stakes tech that could give him leverage against the colonies. We thought he was just a smuggler, but it's way more than that. He's building a network that could destabilize entire settlements if he wanted to."

Rosy sighed, leaning back in her chair. "It's not just about money. He's consolidating power. And if he's distributing this kind of tech, it's not a stretch to think he has buyers who want to use it for more than just profits. This could be a power move—one that could put every colony in danger."

The realization hit them hard. Robusco's reach stretched across planets, from the dense cities on Earth's Moon to the floating stations on Venus. He wasn't just a rogue smuggler; he was a kingpin, orchestrating a black market with technology that could alter the balance of power across the solar system. They exchanged a somber glance, both feeling the weight of what they had stumbled into.

"We're going to need help," Jack finally said, breaking the silence.

Rosy nodded. "But who can we trust with something like this? If Robusco has connections everywhere, we have to be careful who we talk to."

After a moment of thought, Jack looked at her. "Dr. Carson. He's been my mentor for years. He's trustworthy, and he has experience dealing with interplanetary regulations and high-security tech. If anyone can guide us, it's him."

They agreed and decided to meet Dr. Carson in his office after hours. When they arrived, the hallway was deserted, the usual hum of student chatter replaced by an eerie silence. They knocked softly, and Dr. Carson opened the door, his face a mixture of curiosity and concern.

"Jack, Rosy," he greeted them, ushering them inside. "What's this all about? You sounded urgent."

Once inside, they closed the door and took a seat. Jack took a deep breath, glancing at Rosy for reassurance before he began explaining everything. From their initial encounter with Robusco on the Moon, to the encrypted files, the threats they'd faced, and the increasingly unsettling discoveries they had made.

BEYOND THE STARS

As Jack spoke, Dr. Carson's expression shifted from mild interest to intense focus, his brows knitting together. When Jack finally finished, there was a long pause. Dr. Carson took a moment to absorb everything, then leaned back, looking both troubled and impressed.

"Jack, Rosy," he said slowly, his tone somber, "this is... immense. I knew there were rumors about interplanetary smuggling rings, but nothing on this scale. If what you're saying is true, Robusco is not only a threat to the colonies but to Earth itself. He's sitting on a ticking time bomb of tech that, in the wrong hands, could be catastrophic."

Rosy nodded. "That's why we came to you. We need guidance, and we can't afford to go to the authorities just yet. For all we know, Robusco has people on the inside there too."

Dr. Carson nodded gravely. "You did the right thing by coming to me. This is delicate. We have to move quietly if we're going to avoid tipping him off. Let me make some discreet inquiries, and I'll see what resources I can gather without raising suspicion. Meanwhile..." He looked at them seriously. "Promise me you'll be cautious. Robusco has eyes everywhere."

They agreed, grateful for his support. He then set them up with access to a secure communication channel, one that would allow them to exchange information without being traced. It was a relief, and for the first time in weeks, they felt a glimmer of hope. With Dr. Carson's resources and guidance, they could keep digging without constantly looking over their shoulders.

The next day, Jack and Rosy returned to their investigations with renewed determination. Using the secure channel, they gained access to a surveillance network that monitored Robusco's suspected movements across the colonies. Each night, they sifted through data logs, watching Robusco's network and tracking the suspicious shipments that seemed to follow him wherever he went.

Then, one evening, while Jack was combing through a string of messages flagged by Dr. Carson, he stumbled upon a chilling exchange.

It was a coded transmission, intercepted from a private channel, discussing an imminent shipment of banned tech bound for Earth's orbit.

Jack's breath caught. He read the message again, then motioned to Rosy. "Look at this," he whispered, his voice barely above a murmur.

Rosy read the screen, her face draining of color. "He's targeting Earth?"

Jack nodded, his mind racing. "This shipment—it's marked as high-priority and flagged as 'classified equipment for planetary defense.' But I don't think that's the real purpose. If Robusco is planning to move dangerous tech to Earth, he's probably setting up a base there. That would give him a strategic advantage over every colony in the solar system."

They exchanged a worried glance, realizing the stakes were even higher than they'd thought. Robusco's ambitions weren't limited to the outer colonies. If he managed to establish a foothold on Earth, his power would be limitless, his reach stretching to the heart of humanity's home planet.

They spent hours discussing their next move, barely sleeping as they pored over every detail of the intercepted message. Finally, they decided to contact Dr. Carson, knowing this information had to reach him immediately.

In the secure channel, Jack typed out a message to Dr. Carson, relaying what they had discovered. They waited, tense and silent, until a reply came through, instructing them to meet him the next evening.

When they arrived, Dr. Carson's expression was grave. "This changes everything," he said, his voice barely concealing his worry. "If Robusco's next shipment is bound for Earth, this isn't just smuggling. He's positioning himself as a power player, and whatever he's moving could give him the leverage to hold Earth hostage. The authorities need to know, but we can't risk him catching wind of this. We'll need to expose him strategically."

Jack nodded. "So what do we do?"

Dr. Carson thought for a moment, then replied, "We need to intercept that shipment or at the very least, delay it long enough to gather evidence. But it'll be dangerous—if Robusco realizes we're onto him, he won't hesitate to eliminate anyone standing in his way. I'll need to reach out to a few people I trust, and I want you two to keep a low profile. No more unauthorized snooping, and keep communication to this channel only."

Rosy agreed, though Jack could tell she was just as restless as he was, eager to act rather than hide. But they understood the gravity of the situation. They were no longer dealing with an elusive smuggler; they were facing a direct threat to Earth, and the margin for error was razor-thin.

As they returned to their quarters, Jack and Rosy exchanged a solemn look. Their journey had started with curiosity and a shared sense of adventure, but now it had transformed into something far larger and far more dangerous. They had uncovered a conspiracy that could shape the fate of the entire solar system, and they were now the only ones standing in its way.

Rosy took Jack's hand, her gaze steady. "No matter what happens, we're in this together. We started this, and we'll finish it."

Jack squeezed her hand in return, their shared resolve a silent promise in the dim light of their room. They knew the path ahead was fraught with danger, but they were ready. Whatever came next, they would face it side by side, ready to confront the dark forces threatening the future of humanity.

Chapter 13: The Threat Revealed

Jack and Rosy moved cautiously through the dim, sterile halls of the lunar research station. It was late, the usual bustling corridors now empty and eerily quiet. Every footstep echoed, and every flicker of light seemed to make them flinch. After weeks of digging into Robusco's network, they'd finally found a series of leads that connected him to some disturbing findings. They hadn't dared speak about it out loud yet, but the danger felt thicker now, palpable.

Jack turned to Rosy, lowering his voice to barely above a whisper. "Do you feel like...we're being watched?"

Rosy nodded, her brow furrowed. "I thought it was just me. But after everything we've uncovered, I wouldn't be surprised if we've attracted some...unwelcome attention."

A hollow silence hung between them, and they quickened their pace, trying to make their way back to their quarters without incident. But as they passed an isolated section of the research wing, Jack's arm shot out, pulling Rosy to a sudden halt. She followed his gaze, her eyes narrowing on a figure lingering in the shadows, leaning casually against the wall as if waiting for them.

"Can I help you?" Jack called, trying to sound confident, though his heart was hammering in his chest.

The figure straightened and stepped forward, emerging from the shadows. He was a tall man, his face obscured under the brim of a cap, but his posture oozed an unsettling confidence. His eyes glinted as they sized up Jack and Rosy.

"No need for introductions," he said, his voice calm but carrying a razor's edge. "I know exactly who you both are. And I think it's about time you stopped...poking around."

Jack swallowed, his hand tightening slightly around Rosy's. He forced himself to hold the man's gaze. "We're just students," he said evenly, attempting to deflect. "Doing some basic research. Nothing to do with you."

The man chuckled darkly, his eyes flicking over them with a look of disdain. "You think we haven't noticed? Robusco has eyes everywhere, and he doesn't take kindly to little flies buzzing around his affairs." He took a step closer, lowering his voice to a warning. "Drop the questions, stop looking where you shouldn't. If you know what's good for you, that is."

Rosy gripped Jack's hand, and he felt her slight tremor. The man turned on his heel, his words lingering in the air as he walked away, disappearing into the shadows. They remained rooted in place, their minds whirling with the chilling realization that they'd been marked. Only once they were sure the man was gone did they let out the breaths they'd been holding.

"We need to go," Rosy whispered, her voice barely audible.

Jack nodded, guiding her down the hall as they hurried back to the safety of their quarters. He couldn't shake the man's words. The raw edge to his threat, the knowledge that they had finally stepped onto Robusco's radar in a very real way. By the time they reached their quarters, both felt a weight pressing down on them, a silent warning that everything had just changed.

Inside, Jack quickly double-checked the room for any bugs or surveillance devices, just in case. They knew Robusco's network was vast, but they'd underestimated how quickly it would turn its gaze toward them.

"So...now what?" Rosy asked, her voice steadier than her expression. "Do we stop?"

Jack looked at her, his face set with determination. "If we stop now, we're just telling him that he can scare us off with a few threats. Besides, we're in too deep to turn around."

"But what if it's not just threats?" Rosy countered, her eyes filled with concern. "You heard him. They've been watching us, Jack. We can't just brush this off."

Jack took a deep breath, rubbing the back of his neck. "Then we have to be more careful. No more slip-ups. We need to tighten up everything—our communications, our research. We can't let them know our next move."

Rosy sighed, the reality of the situation settling heavily on her shoulders. "You're right. But I can't shake the feeling that this is just the beginning. If Robusco's willing to send someone after us now…"

Jack nodded solemnly, his hand resting on her shoulder. "Then we stay one step ahead. And if we find enough solid evidence, something undeniable, maybe we'll have a chance to take him down before he takes us down."

They spent the rest of the night poring over their recent findings, reviewing every document, every bit of data they'd accumulated. Jack made sure their communications were secure, adding encryption layers to their devices, while Rosy combed through the messages and contacts they'd connected with, double-checking for any leads that might give them an advantage.

Hours passed as they worked in silence, but the tension never left the room. Every now and then, one of them would glance toward the door, half-expecting another visit from one of Robusco's agents. The late-night quiet of the lunar station took on an ominous tone, as if they were no longer within its safe confines but in a labyrinth with eyes on every wall.

As the artificial morning light began filtering into the station, Rosy finally leaned back, rubbing her eyes. "What if this really is too big for us, Jack?" she murmured, the exhaustion clear in her voice.

Jack's gaze softened. "Rosy...if we back down, he'll just keep doing whatever he wants. People will keep getting hurt. I know it feels impossible, but we're closer to the truth than anyone else. If we don't expose him, who will?"

She gave a small, determined nod. "Alright. But let's be careful. We need to watch each other's backs, keep our guard up at all times. If they're watching us, we'll make sure they see exactly what we want them to see."

He offered her a small smile, and for a moment, the tension lifted as they reaffirmed their partnership. "Agreed. We'll be careful," he said, reaching out his hand. She took it, giving it a firm shake, sealing their pact.

They spent the day moving cautiously, avoiding their usual routes and giving each passerby a second look. Every shadow seemed suspicious, every glance prolonged enough to spike their nerves. As they gathered supplies for their next move, they began mapping out an escape plan in case things took a darker turn.

But despite the fear gnawing at them, neither of them was willing to let it deter them. The more they thought about Robusco's operation, the more resolute they became. Jack and Rosy knew they had to keep pushing forward, even if it meant risking everything.

Chapter 14: A Narrow Escape

The dim, cool silence of the lunar corridor settled around Jack and Rosy like a heavy veil. After a long day spent under the scrutinizing eyes of their professors and the vague feeling of someone always watching, the quiet felt comforting. But tonight, an underlying edge made it unsettling.

They moved through the corridor, their steps echoing faintly, trying to maintain composure. Jack kept a firm grip on his datapad, glancing occasionally over his shoulder. They were on their way to Dr. Carson's office to discuss the disturbing threats, but tonight something felt off. As they rounded a corner toward the familiar, well-lit hallway, they froze.

Two figures emerged from the shadows, their faces obscured by cloaks pulled low over their heads. The larger of the two spoke in a low, dangerous voice, "Thought you were clever, didn't you?" The voice held a dark amusement, as if he was relishing the fear they'd ignited in Jack and Rosy.

"Back off," Jack said, but his voice lacked the steel he wanted. The other agent—a shorter, wiry figure—took a step forward.

"We gave you a warning," the man sneered, his voice like gravel. "But maybe you need a stronger reminder." In one swift motion, he lunged toward them. Jack grabbed Rosy's arm, pulling her back, and they stumbled against the wall, the agent's fist narrowly missing Jack's face.

The two agents moved to block their exit, closing in with predatory intent. Jack's heart pounded, his mind racing for an escape. They couldn't fight these men off—not without serious risk—but they knew the station's layout well, every winding path and maintenance tunnel.

Jack tightened his grip on Rosy's hand. "This way!" he shouted, dragging her toward the narrow emergency exit corridor at the far end. They darted past the agents, who cursed and gave chase, their footsteps heavy and echoing.

The chase led them through the cold, sterile underbelly of the station. They veered through dimly lit service tunnels, barely wide enough for the two of them side by side. Jack could hear the agents' harsh breathing growing louder. They turned a corner sharply, sending a stack of crates tumbling into their path to buy a few precious seconds.

"Come on, Rosy, keep up!" Jack urged as they skidded around another bend, the floor slick beneath their feet. He could feel Rosy's grip trembling, her breaths quick and shallow, but she matched his pace.

"Where... are we going?" she panted, her eyes flicking back nervously.

"Dr. Carson's office. We just have to get there," he replied, trying to sound calm, though his heart felt like it would beat right out of his chest. "Once we're inside, we'll be safe."

They found a small, dimly lit alcove near one of the maintenance access doors and ducked inside. Jack leaned against the wall, catching his breath. He could hear the men's footsteps pause just a few feet away. He pressed a finger to his lips, glancing at Rosy, who nodded in understanding. They stood there, barely breathing, as one of the agents growled in frustration, muttering something about "rats slipping through cracks."

After what felt like an eternity, the footsteps receded, but Jack knew they couldn't stay hidden for long. He tugged on Rosy's sleeve, and they made their way, this time in hushed silence, towards Dr. Carson's office.

When they finally reached the door, Jack punched in the access code with trembling fingers. The door slid open, and they stumbled inside, locking it behind them. Dr. Carson looked up, startled, from her work, her face immediately turning pale at the sight of them, disheveled and clearly terrified.

"Jack... Rosy..." She stood and crossed the room quickly, helping them over to a pair of chairs.

Rosy took a shuddering breath. "Dr. Carson, we were... We were followed. They threatened us—said we should stop asking questions." Her voice broke slightly, and she looked to Jack, who nodded grimly.

Dr. Carson's face hardened, her concern deepening. "You were right to come to me. I had hoped you wouldn't get caught up in this kind of danger, but..." She sighed, pacing the room. "If Robusco's men are targeting you now, then you're both at far more risk than I anticipated."

"We can't just let this go, Dr. Carson," Jack said, his voice steady, even defiant. "Not after everything we've learned. If we back off now, he wins. He'll keep smuggling tech, endangering the entire system."

Dr. Carson frowned, considering their words, her gaze sharp and calculating. "It's more than just a game of cat and mouse now, Jack. You're directly in their sights. Robusco doesn't take kindly to interference. I need you both to understand the risk—he's far more powerful than you realize."

"But this just confirms it, doesn't it?" Rosy interjected, her voice firmer now, meeting Dr. Carson's gaze. "If they're willing to intimidate us, it means we're onto something that matters. We're close."

Dr. Carson hesitated, then nodded slowly. "If you're determined to keep going, we need to be smart about this. No more hacking servers or confronting strangers alone. We need a plan that protects you as much as it gathers evidence."

Jack's shoulders relaxed slightly. "What do you suggest?"

Dr. Carson glanced at the locked door, then lowered her voice. "From here on, we operate quietly. I have contacts within certain sectors—those who might help us anonymously without putting you in danger. I'll also give you both access to the encrypted network. Any information you gather, you'll upload there, and I'll ensure it reaches trusted authorities."

Rosy breathed a small sigh of relief. "Thank you, Dr. Carson. We... we were beginning to feel like we were alone in this."

Dr. Carson placed a comforting hand on Rosy's shoulder. "You're not alone, but remember: Robusco is ruthless. This isn't something to take lightly."

Jack nodded, glancing at Rosy, a new resolve lighting up in his eyes. "Then we'll do whatever it takes to bring him down. He thinks he can scare us, but he's only made us more determined."

Dr. Carson gave him a cautious smile. "Just promise me you'll be careful. Remember, your safety is the priority. This isn't just a fight for justice—it's a fight to protect yourselves."

As they left Dr. Carson's office, Jack and Rosy walked in silence, a new sense of purpose guiding their steps. They were scared—terrified, even—but they understood the stakes now. Robusco's threats had done nothing but strengthen their resolve. The chase had begun, and this time, they wouldn't run.

Chapter 15: The Decision to Act

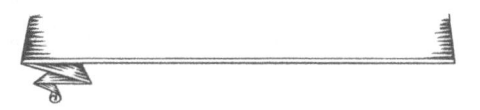

Jack and Rosy sat in Dr. Carson's dimly lit office, the faint hum of the station outside barely cutting through the heavy silence that had settled over them. Their evidence, meticulously gathered over countless sleepless nights, lay scattered across Dr. Carson's desk. Images, decrypted messages, and schematics of shipments—all pointing to Robusco's smuggling operation—felt like a mountain of proof to them, but they both knew the real challenge lay ahead.

Dr. Carson cleared her throat, breaking the silence. "You're both absolutely certain you want to go through with this?" Her gaze was sharp, flicking between them with something akin to motherly worry.

Jack nodded firmly, his face set in determined lines. "We're certain. Robusco's operation goes far beyond petty smuggling. This tech... it could disrupt everything we've worked for in interplanetary cooperation. He's destabilizing entire colonies. We can't ignore that."

Rosy's gaze softened as she watched him, his passion and sense of responsibility palpable. "We're in this together," she said softly. "If we don't take action, who will?"

Dr. Carson gave a resigned nod. "Then I've arranged a meeting with an officer I trust in the Lunar Security Division. She's known for her integrity and has handled sensitive cases before. I can't guarantee she'll agree with you, but she'll at least hear you out."

The next morning, Jack and Rosy walked into the tall, imposing headquarters of the Lunar Security Division, located in one of the central domes of the station. The clean, metallic walls and polished floors seemed cold and unwelcoming as they approached the front desk. Every official they passed wore crisp uniforms, eyes flicking between data screens and bustling officers, as if to remind them of the sheer scale of what they were up against.

Dr. Carson had instructed them to ask for Lieutenant Mira Chen, a veteran in the field and known for her unyielding dedication to justice. The receptionist, a serious young man with a badge identifying him as Officer Holden, studied them with a cool gaze as they explained their purpose.

"Lieutenant Chen will see you," he said finally, pointing them toward a waiting room.

They didn't wait long. A tall, formidable woman with sharp eyes and graying hair entered, her presence filling the room. She extended a hand as she introduced herself. "Lieutenant Mira Chen. Dr. Carson speaks highly of you both."

"Thank you for agreeing to see us, Lieutenant," Jack said, standing up and shaking her hand. "We have evidence of a large-scale smuggling operation. It's more than just illegal tech—it's endangering colonies and the very stability of our interplanetary network."

Lieutenant Chen's gaze flickered to the folder of evidence they carried. "Let's see it."

They laid everything out for her: images, intercepted communications, logs from the Lunar research center, and even the decrypted messages they had risked so much to obtain. Lieutenant Chen examined each piece carefully, nodding along as they explained their findings. For a moment, Jack felt a glimmer of hope.

But as she reached the end of the stack, Lieutenant Chen closed the folder and leaned back, her expression unreadable. "This is compelling, but it's also… difficult to verify. Without corroborative eyewitnesses or confirmed samples of the tech you're claiming is being smuggled, this could be taken as conjecture. I'm not saying you're wrong," she added, seeing the protest forming on Jack's lips, "but we need airtight proof to pursue a case this serious."

Rosy leaned forward, desperation in her eyes. "Lieutenant, you have to understand, we've done everything we can with the resources we have. This isn't just conjecture; Robusco's operation is putting lives at risk. We know he has connections within the Division, or at least officials turning a blind eye. We're risking our lives by even bringing this to you."

Lieutenant Chen looked at them both thoughtfully. She opened her mouth as if to respond, but at that moment, the door opened, and another officer entered. His gaze darted suspiciously between Jack, Rosy, and the Lieutenant before he leaned in close to Chen, whispering something in her ear.

When the officer left, Chen's demeanor had changed subtly, her eyes narrowing with caution. She cleared her throat. "You've taken significant risks, and I don't doubt your commitment," she said slowly, choosing her words carefully. "But it would be wise to consider your position carefully. There are... complexities within the division that might not work in your favor."

Jack's face paled slightly, frustration and confusion battling in his expression. "So, you're saying we're on our own? That you won't do anything?"

Lieutenant Chen hesitated. "I'm saying that without irrefutable evidence, my hands are tied. If I were to pursue this with what you've provided and without my department's full backing, it could jeopardize more than just your safety. I suggest you let this go."

Stunned, Jack sat back, feeling as though the ground had been ripped from beneath him. He looked to Rosy, whose face mirrored his disbelief. The Lieutenant rose, glancing at them with a hint of regret in her eyes before gesturing to the door.

"Thank you for coming forward," she said quietly. "If there's anything further you come across, my door remains open." And with that, she left them, leaving the bitter taste of disappointment hanging in the air.

They walked out of the headquarters in silence, the hum of the station's bustling streets feeling strangely muted. The one place they'd hoped would be an ally had turned its back on them. Jack clenched his fists, his gaze hardening.

"So that's it?" he muttered under his breath. "The authorities won't do anything. They'd rather stay comfortable than do what's right."

Rosy placed a hand on his shoulder, her voice low but firm. "Then we'll go to someone who will listen."

Jack looked at her, caught off guard. "Who? If the authorities won't touch this, who else is there?"

"Public exposure," she replied. "There are independent media networks, investigative reporters who would jump on a story like this. If we can't get justice through the system, we'll shine a light on this ourselves. We're not giving up."

A sense of hope crept back into Jack's mind, but with it came a twinge of fear. Going public would place them directly in Robusco's line of fire. Still, Rosy's determination and the quiet resolve in her gaze sparked something in him. They had come too far to turn back now.

They returned to Dr. Carson's office, explaining what had happened. She listened quietly, a deep frown etching across her face. When they finished, she sighed, her fingers steepled thoughtfully.

"So, you're certain you want to take this public?" she asked, her gaze piercing.

Jack and Rosy exchanged a glance, then nodded. "We don't have any other choice," Rosy said, her voice resolute. "If we back down now, Robusco's operation will only grow. We owe it to everyone he's hurt and endangered."

Dr. Carson leaned back in her chair, assessing them both carefully. "Then I'll support you. There's a journalist I know who works with

BEYOND THE STARS

Lunar Independent Media—she's trustworthy and has a reputation for taking on cases no one else will touch."

Dr. Carson pulled up a secure channel and typed a quick message. "Her name is Alana Reyes. I'll arrange a meeting. But remember, once this goes public, there's no turning back. Robusco will retaliate—hard."

Jack felt a shiver run down his spine but nodded, his jaw set. "We know the risks. We're ready."

Later that night, as he and Rosy returned to their quarters, he glanced at her, feeling a rush of gratitude. She gave him a small smile, a silent acknowledgment of everything they'd been through and everything still to come.

"Tomorrow's a new chapter," he murmured as they reached their door.

Rosy nodded, a fire in her eyes. "Then let's make sure it's one they'll never forget."

Chapter 16: Unconventional Allies

Jack and Rosy moved through the dimly lit hallways of the university, their footsteps echoing softly in the early morning quiet. The decision to enlist the help of their AI professors wasn't one they'd taken lightly, and both felt the weight of it as they neared Dr. Verity's lab. The campus, with its sprawling lunar architecture and modern, angular design, was typically bustling with students, but today it felt like a shadowy maze, every corner hiding potential threats. After their close encounters with Robusco's agents, they'd grown wary of being watched. Jack found himself glancing over his shoulder, while Rosy held her tablet close, clutched like a lifeline.

Inside the lab, Dr. Verity waited, her robotic form as still as a statue until they entered. A tall, slender figure, Dr. Verity had a minimalist humanoid appearance, with bright cerulean optics that adjusted to the lighting as they walked in. Her head tilted slightly, signaling her awareness of their entrance.

"Jack. Rosy. I've been expecting you," she greeted, her voice smooth and resonant, with a cadence that was both calming and commanding.

Rosy offered a faint smile. "We hoped you might. We didn't know where else to turn."

Dr. Verity observed them both closely, her optics flickering. "Dr. Carson's message was brief, but I understand you're engaged in a risky endeavor. I can assume this pertains to Robusco?"

Jack and Rosy exchanged a glance before Jack replied, "Yes. He's been running a black-market tech smuggling operation, and we're certain he has connections on several planets. But our evidence isn't enough. Every time we get close, something happens. We're being followed. Watched."

Dr. Verity nodded once, processing. "Such suspicions are valid. It's likely that Robusco's network extends across educational, governmental, and even security channels. Any overt approach to expose him may put you in immediate danger."

Rosy stepped forward. "That's why we need your help, Dr. Verity. And Dr. Orion's, if he's willing."

The lights in the lab dimmed momentarily as Dr. Verity's processors activated an encrypted communication line. "Let me contact Dr. Orion. I believe he'll find this... interesting."

A few seconds later, Dr. Orion's voice crackled over the speakers, smooth and rich, though with a slight distortion. "Dr. Verity. Jack, Rosy. I understand you're in need of my expertise?"

Jack shifted nervously, nodding. "We've uncovered evidence of Robusco's network, but we're at a dead end. We need a way to track his movements in real time. To connect the dots."

Dr. Orion let out a mechanical hum, one that always seemed to signal he was intrigued. "I'm in. But first, you'll need to agree to specific protocols. If Robusco has compromised the university's standard communication channels, we must use secure servers. And I suggest adopting aliases."

With the gravity of the situation sinking in, Jack and Rosy agreed, setting up new identities within Dr. Verity's secure system. Rosy chose "Lyra," after her favorite constellation, while Jack settled on "Ares," for the god of courage.

"We'll begin by monitoring data packets linked to shipping routes," Dr. Orion continued. "We need to identify patterns in Robusco's supply chain—starting with recent activities on Mars and Venus, where smuggling routes have already been flagged."

BEYOND THE STARS

Jack leaned in, eyes wide with determination. "And if we track his supply chain? Then what?"

Dr. Verity's optics glowed a shade brighter. "With my access to legal databases and interplanetary law enforcement files, I'll be able to validate any findings and possibly expose the gaps he exploits in customs and security channels. We'll need tangible proof of his operations, including cargo manifests, docking schedules, and personnel logs."

Rosy was listening intently, nodding along. "We've been cautious, but... this feels like the first time we have a real chance at stopping him."

"Caution is key," Dr. Orion's voice intoned, his deep resonance filling the room. "Any misstep, and Robusco's network could retaliate."

Dr. Verity adjusted her stance, looking directly at them. "Let me teach you both about masking your digital trails. I'll run you through essential encryption methods to use on your devices. And for extra precaution, we'll set up a series of proxy servers across several planetary networks."

For hours, Jack and Rosy learned the intricate methods of data encryption and digital stealth, their fingers moving across screens under Dr. Verity and Dr. Orion's guidance. They felt their understanding deepen, a quiet confidence growing. They weren't just students now—they were partners in a cause that had grown beyond them.

As the days went on, they fell into a steady rhythm of secretive meetings and late-night conversations. They poured over files, connecting shipments and supply routes, and piecing together a web of connections that stretched farther than they had ever imagined. It was during one of these late nights, as the glow of the data monitors cast shadows across their faces, that Jack looked over at Rosy.

"Lyra," he murmured, her alias feeling strangely natural on his lips. "We've been at this for weeks, barely sleeping... are you sure you're still with me?"

She looked back at him, her eyes softening. "There's no place else I'd rather be, Ares." Her hand reached out, hesitating for a moment before resting on his. "We're in this together, Jack. For as long as it takes."

They stayed like that, in quiet understanding, for just a moment before returning to their work. Dr. Verity watched from her station, her optics flickering, as if understanding the significance of the silent exchange.

Then, one evening, Dr. Orion called them both to his lab with news. "I've intercepted communications suggesting that Robusco's network is making preparations for a massive shipment, with a significant portion bound for Earth orbit. The time to act may be sooner than we expected."

Jack and Rosy shared a determined look, their resolve only deepening. They were on the edge of something monumental, and they knew that, with the support of Dr. Verity and Dr. Orion, they finally had a fighting chance.

The alliance was unconventional, built on trust in the most unlikely of allies. But in those quiet, dimly lit labs, amidst screens glowing with encrypted data, Jack and Rosy felt hope—hope that they could change the course of something far bigger than themselves.

Chapter 17: The Heart of the Network

In the soft hum of Dr. Orion's lab, Jack and Rosy sat side by side, eyes fixed on the screens in front of them. The glow of data illuminated their faces, casting shadows that seemed to dance in sync with the lines of code flashing on the monitors. They were deep within Robusco's network now, each keystroke bringing them closer to the heart of his operations. The resources provided by Dr. Orion and Dr. Verity had opened doors that otherwise would have been impossible to enter, allowing them access to layers of information that painted a far darker picture than either of them had anticipated.

Jack broke the silence, his voice hushed yet tense. "Look at this," he said, pointing at the display. "It's not just tech suppliers and smugglers. These connections go right into administrative sectors on Mars, Venus... even the Earth Council's orbital division."

Rosy leaned closer, her eyes widening as she absorbed the scope of what they were seeing. "I can't believe this. He's got people everywhere, influencing decisions, overseeing shipments. He's been building this for years."

Dr. Verity's voice echoed softly from the speakers, her smooth tone reassuring. "What you're seeing is the work of someone who's very good at remaining hidden. Robusco has layers of separation between himself and his network. It will be difficult to reach him directly."

Jack ran a hand through his hair, feeling the strain of their sleepless nights but unwilling to step away. "Then we go through each layer, no matter how long it takes."

Dr. Orion's low voice chimed in. "I can initiate algorithmic analysis on the data points you've uncovered. We should be able to chart out the high-priority nodes—those that could expose Robusco's operations more publicly."

Rosy turned to Jack, her eyes bright despite the exhaustion he knew she felt. "It's risky, but if we can intercept the communications coming from these high-priority points, it might force him to alter his plans... or even pull back."

Jack nodded, his resolve strengthening. "It's a start. And if we're lucky, it'll shake things up enough to make him slip."

Hours turned into days, each one blurring into the next as Jack and Rosy delved deeper, connecting points on a sprawling web of corruption that stretched from the far reaches of Mars to the bustling mining colonies on Ganymede. They worked in tandem, each anticipating the other's moves and filling in gaps without needing to explain. Jack found himself marveling at her focus and her quick thinking, the way she could piece together information with an almost intuitive sense.

One night, as they took a rare break to recharge and grab some food from the cafeteria, they found themselves sitting alone in a quiet corner. The silence was comfortable, an unspoken bond between them as they finally looked up from the screens and into each other's tired faces.

Rosy took a sip from her coffee, wrapping her hands around the cup to warm them. "You know, I think we've been at this for almost 72 hours straight. How are you holding up?"

Jack chuckled softly, his own coffee untouched. "Honestly? I'm exhausted. But it's worth it." He glanced over at her, a smile touching his lips. "Besides, I couldn't do this without you."

Her cheeks flushed slightly, and she looked away, trying to hide her smile. "I think you could. But... I'm glad we're in this together." There was a brief silence before she added, her voice soft, "This is probably the craziest thing I've ever done."

Jack leaned back, studying her face. "Me too. And we're risking everything. But you're... well, you're kind of amazing, Rosy."

She looked at him, meeting his gaze fully, and for a moment, the noise and stress of their mission faded away. It was just them, two people pulled together by fate and circumstance, finding a rare moment of clarity in the chaos. She gave a soft laugh, breaking the tension with her usual warmth.

"Alright, partner," she said, tapping his shoulder playfully. "Let's get back to work before we end up falling asleep here."

They returned to the lab, but that moment lingered, a silent promise between them that bolstered their determination as they continued to unravel Robusco's web. Each new discovery fueled their drive, and the long hours of shared struggle seemed to bring them even closer, forging a connection neither of them had expected.

Late one evening, Jack stumbled across a message that set off alarms in his mind. "Rosy, look at this," he called out, his voice tense. She rushed over, her eyes scanning the intercepted communication.

"An unscheduled shipment heading to one of the mining colonies in the asteroid belt?" she muttered, her brow furrowing. "It's coded as 'medical supplies,' but that ID tag... it matches the ones we flagged as potential smuggling shipments."

Jack's fingers flew across the keyboard, opening a secure channel to Dr. Orion. "Dr. Orion, can you cross-reference this ID with recent cargo manifests from Robusco's network?"

"Working on it," Dr. Orion replied, the sound of his processors whirring in the background. "Ah... confirmed. This shipment isn't just unscheduled. It's listed under a fictitious supplier linked to Robusco's network."

Rosy clenched her fists, her jaw set in frustration. "So he's moving something big. Probably through every loophole he's crafted along the way."

Jack gave her a determined look. "Then we follow it. This could be the break we need."

For the next few hours, they tracked the shipment's progress, analyzing its route through various checkpoints, and monitoring any communication linked to its transport. They grew more certain that the shipment was crucial to Robusco's operation, possibly carrying something that could make or break his network.

As the night stretched on, they became aware of how isolated they were in their small corner of the lunar station, their only allies the two AI professors and each other. The intensity of their mission had formed a rhythm, a familiar cadence that made them both feel as though they'd been working side by side for far longer than a few weeks. And yet, beneath the exhaustion, there was a growing sense of connection, an understanding that had been forged in the late hours and whispered conversations in empty hallways.

Finally, as they sat back, satisfied with the progress they'd made, Rosy turned to Jack, her eyes soft but determined. "We're in this deeper than we ever planned, aren't we?"

Jack met her gaze, his own expression equally resolved. "Yeah. But I don't regret any of it. Not a single moment." He paused, then added, "And no matter what happens, I'm glad we're in it together."

She reached out, her hand resting on his for a brief, unspoken moment. "Same here, Jack."

The words held a quiet promise, a resilience that neither of them had voiced but both understood. They would see this through, no matter the cost.

With a shared look of resolve, they returned to their screens, diving back into the world of encrypted messages and hidden transactions, ready to bring down the network they'd worked so hard to infiltrate.

BEYOND THE STARS

The heart of Robusco's empire was within reach, and together, they were prepared to face whatever came next.

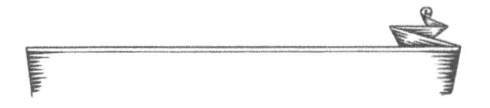

Chapter 18: Strength in Unity

In the dim glow of Dr. Verity's lab, Jack and Rosy huddled over their monitors, watching as lines of encrypted data streamed across the screens. They'd grown used to the late nights and quiet intensity that filled these hours, knowing each moment brought them closer to unraveling the heart of Robusco's empire. But tonight was different. They'd found something—or rather, someone.

The message had arrived just minutes ago, appearing as a secure, anonymous link from an unknown source. Dr. Orion had quickly verified its origin and confirmed it was a direct feed from an independent network. Now, as they read the short message, they felt a mixture of intrigue and tension building between them.

Rosy's brow furrowed as she scanned the cryptic text again. "Who do you think this 'Nova' is? And how could they know what we're working on?"

Jack shrugged, though his mind raced with theories. "If Nova's been intercepting and sabotaging Robusco's shipments, they're probably plugged into some of the same networks we've been probing. Could be an ex-insider... or another rogue operator."

Dr. Verity's soft, metallic voice filled the room, her tone both analytical and encouraging. "It's possible that Nova has access to high-level encryption tools. Their methods are precise, and their timing has consistently disrupted Robusco's logistical channels."

"So they're one step ahead, and they're helping us by default," Rosy mused, a glint of excitement in her eyes. She tapped the screen thoughtfully. "What if we respond? We need allies, and Nova might be the perfect fit."

Jack studied the message one last time, then glanced at Rosy with a determined smile. "I'm with you. Let's see what they want."

He typed a quick reply, and they waited in silence, their breaths held in anticipation. Moments later, a response flashed onto the screen, simple and direct:

Nova here. I know what you're after. Let's work together—secure comms only.

Jack and Rosy exchanged glances, a silent understanding passing between them. Dr. Orion swiftly integrated a secure channel for their communication, adding layers of encryption to mask their identities. Within minutes, they were online with Nova.

The screen lit up with Nova's first message: I've been following Robusco for years. He's dangerous, and he's getting bolder. If you're serious about stopping him, I can provide intel—locations, contacts, security measures. But there's a catch.

Rosy leaned forward, typing back quickly. We're listening. What's the catch?

There was a pause before Nova's reply came through, concise and to the point. I need full access to your findings. We'll work in tandem, but everything you know, I need to know.

Jack exhaled, casting a cautious glance at Rosy. "This person is asking for a lot. We've been so careful with who we share information with…"

Rosy nodded, understanding the weight of his hesitation. But then her expression softened. "I think we have to trust someone, Jack. And if Nova's as deep in Robusco's network as they seem, we'll have an advantage we didn't have before."

She turned to Dr. Verity. "What do you think?"

Dr. Verity's voice came through smoothly, her circuits humming softly. "Trust in this context is a calculated risk. However, Nova's

BEYOND THE STARS

history of sabotaging Robusco's shipments suggests alignment with your goals. Their resources could indeed expedite your mission."

Jack finally nodded, typing out their agreement to share intel. Immediately, Nova's response came through with detailed lists of Robusco's recent transactions and schedules for shipments across various points in the solar system. The files included contacts, encrypted communication logs, and a map of Robusco's active bases—information so detailed, it took Jack and Rosy several minutes to process the enormity of what they were seeing.

One last thing, Nova added after a pause. You're not safe. Robusco's security detected movement near his shipment lines. They may suspect a mole.

Rosy felt a chill run down her spine. "So he's already onto us," she murmured, glancing nervously at Jack. "We'll need to be more careful from here on out."

The weight of their situation settled heavily on them both. Despite the layers of encryption and firewalls, despite Dr. Orion's careful monitoring, they knew that Robusco's reach extended farther than they could predict. But with Nova, they finally had a foothold.

Over the next few days, they worked closely with Nova, using the AI professors' networks to create complex algorithms for tracking shipments and establishing hidden links between Robusco's contacts. Each new connection brought them closer to the center of Robusco's operation, piecing together a structure of corruption, bribery, and deception that touched almost every major colony in the solar system.

The sleepless nights and quiet, intense conversations continued. And as they shared more moments in the quiet of the lab, Jack and Rosy found themselves becoming more than partners in a mission—they were partners in something deeper, something that seemed to grow stronger each time they met a new challenge together.

One evening, after hours of cross-referencing coordinates and communications logs, they took a rare break. Rosy leaned back in her chair, stretching her arms above her head. "It feels like we're finally getting somewhere, doesn't it?"

Jack nodded, smiling softly as he watched her. "I couldn't have done this without you, Rosy. I don't think I would've made it this far alone."

She smiled back, a warmth in her eyes that he hadn't seen before. "Me neither. You know, when we first started this, I didn't know what to expect. But now, I feel like we're… I don't know, unstoppable."

He reached over, squeezing her hand gently. "Then let's finish this. Together."

Their quiet moment was interrupted by a ping from the secure channel—they had another message from Nova.

Intercepted message: Nova typed, attaching an encrypted file. Robusco's planning a major move. High-profile shipment. We'll need to coordinate if we're going to stop this one.

As they opened the file, they saw the manifest listed under the innocuous label AgriTech Supplies. But they both knew what this meant. The shipment likely contained something far more dangerous, concealed under layers of bureaucratic approval.

Jack looked at Rosy, his face resolute. "This is it. If we can expose this shipment, we'll have enough to take Robusco down."

Rosy met his gaze, a fierce determination lighting her eyes. "Then let's do it. We've come too far to back down now."

In the hours that followed, they worked tirelessly, coordinating their next steps with Nova while keeping Dr. Verity and Dr. Orion in the loop. The AI professors offered additional resources, scanning incoming and outgoing logs from Robusco's central hub and alerting Jack and Rosy to any suspicious patterns. Together, their team of allies—some human, some not—felt unstoppable.

As they prepared for the final stages of their plan, Rosy paused, glancing at Jack with a smile. "You know, if this works, we'll probably be famous."

Jack laughed, the tension easing for a moment. "Maybe. But honestly? I'd settle for seeing Robusco taken down for good."

She nodded, her expression softening. "Me too."

They stood together, ready to face the trials that lay ahead, feeling stronger and more united than ever. For the first time, they felt as though they truly had a chance—an opportunity to make a real difference and to bring justice to the colonies. With Nova's intelligence, the AI professors' guidance, and each other, they knew they had what they needed to finally confront Robusco's empire and end his reign once and for all.

Chapter 19: The Mars Mission

Jack leaned back in his chair, exhaling as the final map of Robusco's headquarters loaded onto the screen. Mars wasn't just a different planet; it was a fortress of its own, with a culture, ecosystem, and security system unlike anything they had encountered so far. Rosy sat across from him, poring over the data in silence, her face illuminated by the soft glow of the screen.

"So this is it," Jack murmured, breaking the silence. "Robusco's entire network, tucked away in Mars's industrial complex."

"Feels surreal, doesn't it?" Rosy replied, her eyes still scanning the layout. "We've come so far... yet now it feels like everything could go wrong with just one misstep."

Dr. Verity's soothing, synthetic voice interrupted, filling the small room. "Jack, Rosy, I've identified all points of entry and the potential risks associated with each. Robusco's main base is layered with high-level security, from bio-scanners to AI-synced drones. It won't be easy, but I believe you have a viable chance if you're careful."

Jack raised an eyebrow. "If we're careful. That's reassuring."

Dr. Orion, always the realist, interjected. "There's no margin for error here. As soon as you breach the complex, you'll have roughly thirty minutes before the security system triggers full lockdown protocols. Robusco's AI security division is set up to detect any irregularities, which means the slightest disruption could blow your cover."

"So, no pressure," Rosy quipped, her voice tinged with nervous energy. She glanced over at Jack, who offered her a reassuring smile.

Nova's message blinked on-screen, text scrolling across quickly. "Trust me, you won't be going in blind. I've managed to access a few of their system weak spots remotely. I'll be providing live support and feeding you updates in real time."

Jack tapped a response. "Thanks, Nova. We'll be counting on you for this."

After a long pause, Dr. Verity's voice came back, gentler this time. "I know this won't be easy, but you two are the best chance we have. If Robusco isn't stopped now, his operations will spread unchecked across the colonies. Your mission is more than a disruption—it's a stand for what's left of our interplanetary integrity."

Jack nodded, knowing the weight of those words. Every step they'd taken had led to this moment. "We're not backing down now."

Rosy's hand moved to Jack's shoulder, and for a moment, they just shared a silent resolve. They both knew what they were risking, but they had made it through so much already; to turn back now would mean abandoning everyone who was counting on them.

The next few days passed in a whirlwind of preparation. Dr. Orion drilled them on the specifics of Mars's complex security protocols, which were almost alien in their rigidity. Every entry point required a layer of clearance that could only be bypassed through false identities. Rosy had become 'Carla Montrose,' a tech contractor with a specialty in system diagnostics, while Jack became 'Ryan Stone,' a logistics coordinator brought in to oversee efficiency in Mars's ever-growing tech manufacturing sector.

"Remember, you'll need to maintain your aliases constantly," Dr. Verity warned them during one late-night training session. "Your entry identities have to hold up under even the most casual scrutiny. I've programmed a basic background for each of you, but it's up to you to fill in the blanks if questioned."

BEYOND THE STARS

Rosy nodded, practicing her "Carla Montrose" accent in front of the mirror as Jack laughed. "It's not bad," he admitted, "but try sounding like you're slightly disinterested in everything. You're a tech contractor, not a revolutionary."

She tossed a mock glare at him. "Thanks, Ryan. Good to know you're fully embracing your 'logistics' persona."

The training became grueling as the days wore on, and exhaustion was a constant companion. But Jack and Rosy pushed forward, honing their skills and mastering every aspect of the infiltration plan. The professors simulated different crisis scenarios, drilling them to respond with precision and composure. Jack practiced disarming alarms while Rosy worked on bypassing bio-scanners, their every move watched over by Dr. Verity and Dr. Orion.

Finally, the day of departure arrived. As they packed their equipment, Nova sent a final message.

"All comm channels have been encrypted. You'll be receiving real-time updates through a secure line. Stay alert, and remember: I'm with you."

Dr. Verity added, "Once you're within Mars's airspace, we'll temporarily lose direct connection. Maintain protocol until you reach the designated base. We'll be monitoring your movements as best as possible from here."

The professors' last words stayed with them as they boarded the spacecraft. The journey to Mars was quiet, tense. Jack could see the determination etched on Rosy's face, her jaw set as she gazed out the window. He reached over, taking her hand.

"You ready for this?" he asked softly.

Rosy nodded, squeezing his hand. "I have to be. For everyone relying on us... and for us."

They arrived on Mars under the cover of false identities and a scheduled drop for new tech contractors. The industrial sector was as stark and imposing as they had imagined, with colossal metal structures looming in every direction and a pervasive haze that gave the entire area a sense of secrecy and tension. As they walked through the main terminal, Jack felt a chill—this was Robusco's domain, the heart of his empire, and they were walking right into it.

They checked into their temporary quarters, a small, windowless unit that suited their purposes perfectly. It was close enough to the industrial complex that they could get in and out quickly if needed. Jack wasted no time pulling up their first point of infiltration, a concealed access door marked only for "Authorized Personnel."

Rosy glanced around, ensuring they were alone. "So, this is it."

Jack nodded. "We stick to the plan. No deviations unless absolutely necessary."

Taking a deep breath, they both steeled themselves. With one last check to confirm their equipment was secure, they slipped into the shadows of Mars's industrial maze, each step taking them closer to Robusco's lair and, potentially, the most dangerous mission of their lives.

Back at the university, Dr. Verity and Dr. Orion monitored their movements, their screens lit up with data feeds tracking every second of Jack and Rosy's approach. Dr. Orion's voice, calm yet vigilant, reached them through their earpieces.

"Jack, Rosy, we're losing direct contact as you enter restricted zones. Remember the protocol and stay alert. We'll re-establish communication once you've reached the safe zone."

Jack felt a surge of adrenaline. There would be no more hand-holding from here on out; it was up to them now.

With a last glance at each other, they moved deeper into the complex, slipping past checkpoints with the ease of their new identities. The mission had officially begun, and each step was a reminder that there was no turning back now.

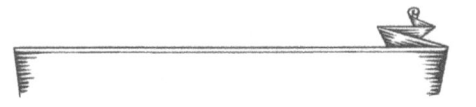

Chapter 20: Creating the Diversion

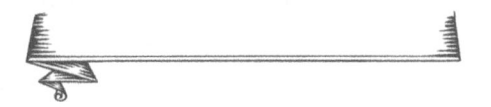

The air inside Mars's industrial zone felt thick and heavy as Jack and Rosy moved quickly through the narrow, dimly lit passageways. The constant thrum of machinery was interrupted by the occasional hiss of steam pipes, giving the complex a faintly oppressive atmosphere. They pulled their hoods up and kept their heads low as they approached the meeting point where they'd find Nova's contacts.

"How do we know they're trustworthy?" Rosy whispered, her voice barely audible over the background noise.

Jack shrugged, glancing over his shoulder. "We don't. But Nova's pulled through for us so far. If we're going to pull this off, we're going to need them."

Ahead of them, a figure emerged from the shadows. Short and wiry, with a scar cutting across his cheek, he gave them a quick nod, then jerked his head toward a small alleyway. Jack and Rosy exchanged a glance before following him.

"Name's Zane," he said curtly, his voice gravelly. "Nova tells me you're looking to make a little noise around here. You got the gear?"

Rosy patted her pack. "Enough to cause the outage we discussed. You sure you've got everything else covered?"

Zane grinned, revealing a chipped tooth. "You just worry about getting in and out. My people have set up blockades around the perimeter. Once the power goes, everyone will be too busy dealing with 'malfunctions' to notice you two slipping in."

Another ally stepped forward, a woman in her thirties with bright, calculating eyes. "I'm Lena. I'll be handling remote surveillance—keeping an eye on Mars's local security networks. If anyone even sneezes near the power grid, I'll know."

With everything in place, they reviewed the plan one last time. The power outage would disrupt a sizable portion of the industrial district, throwing the area into temporary chaos and triggering emergency protocols across the sector. It would last for just a few minutes, enough time for them to enter Robusco's compound undetected.

As they finished prepping the last of the devices, Dr. Verity's voice crackled in their earpieces. "Jack, Rosy, everything is synchronized on our end. When the signal goes live, you'll have approximately four minutes until backup generators restore the main systems. You'll need to move quickly."

Jack adjusted his earpiece. "Understood. We're ready here."

With a nod, Zane activated the power disruption sequence. Jack and Rosy felt the ground vibrate slightly as power lines surged and electrical systems sputtered.

"Go!" Zane hissed, waving them forward.

Jack and Rosy darted through the alley, their footsteps barely audible in the now eerily silent corridor. The lights in the compound flickered before going dark, casting the industrial sector into an inky blackness broken only by the faint glow of emergency lights. Alarms began blaring in the distance as workers and security personnel scrambled to respond to the power failure.

Dr. Orion's voice guided them through the labyrinthine hallways. "You're about two hundred meters from the main checkpoint. Take the left corridor up ahead. Security cameras are temporarily disabled, but you'll need to hurry."

They reached the checkpoint just as a group of confused guards rushed past, too preoccupied to notice them slipping into the secure corridor. Each step brought them deeper into Robusco's domain, the

BEYOND THE STARS

heart of his smuggling empire. Jack's pulse quickened as they passed rows of locked storage containers and secured data terminals.

"Almost there," Dr. Verity whispered in their ears. "Another fifty meters."

The air felt colder here, the corridors lined with thick, steel-reinforced walls. They passed through another checkpoint and into a cavernous storage area lined with server banks and surveillance monitors. This was where Robusco kept the records of his operations—shipment logs, personnel lists, and possibly even the names of his clients.

Jack and Rosy exchanged a tense glance, each of them aware that this was the culmination of everything they'd worked for.

"Nova, do you have access to the internal system?" Jack whispered into his mic.

"Already plugged in," came Nova's voice. "I've set up a data siphon; just plug into any of the mainframes, and it'll start pulling everything we need."

Jack moved toward the central console, inserting Nova's encrypted drive. The screen flickered to life, a series of files and codes flashing rapidly as the data transfer began.

"Three minutes left before the power stabilizes," Dr. Orion warned. "Prepare for any signs of system override."

Just as the last file uploaded, an alarm sounded, blaring louder and closer than before. Rosy's eyes widened as she checked her watch. "We're out of time—they've noticed us!"

Dr. Verity's calm voice filtered through the chaos. "Don't panic. Exit through the west corridor and move up two floors. Lena's just confirmed that reinforcements are delayed, but you'll need to be quick."

The west corridor led them into a narrow passageway filled with old maintenance equipment. They hurried down the hall, but as they rounded a corner, they heard the unmistakable sound of footsteps approaching rapidly from behind.

"Hold on!" Zane's voice crackled over the comm. "Blocking the hallways with some 'maintenance delays' on the system. Keep moving forward; I'll stall them for as long as I can."

Rosy glanced back, her eyes darting with worry. "How much longer until we're clear?"

"We're almost there," Jack whispered, gripping her hand as they moved forward. The tension between them was thick, their hearts pounding in sync. A flash of light came from behind, followed by a shout as one of Robusco's guards spotted them.

"Stop right there!"

Without thinking, Jack pulled Rosy into a side alcove, holding his breath as the guards rushed past, oblivious to their presence. The noise of their footsteps faded, and Jack and Rosy exchanged a look of relief before slipping out and continuing down the corridor.

Nova's voice came back over the earpiece. "Security is converging near the main entrance. Zane and Lena are redirecting them, but it won't hold for long. Finish up, fast."

They reached the final security door, their escape route leading back to the main industrial entrance. Jack keyed in the access code Lena had provided, and the door slid open just as the lights flickered back to full strength, signaling the end of their precious window.

"Let's go," Jack urged, pulling Rosy through the door just as the lights fully reactivated, and the power resumed in the complex.

The compound roared back to life, and they could hear voices shouting orders nearby. They sprinted down the hallway, the exit finally in sight. They were almost clear when a voice echoed over the loudspeakers.

"Attention: Unauthorized access detected in the data storage area. All units proceed to lockdown. Intruders are attempting to breach the premises."

"Guess that's us," Jack muttered, picking up the pace.

BEYOND THE STARS

The exit loomed ahead, and they dashed toward it, adrenaline fueling each step. Zane and Lena were already outside, motioning them forward. They managed to slip through the door just as it locked shut behind them, sealing off the building.

"Close one," Zane said with a grin. "You two sure know how to stir up trouble."

Jack laughed breathlessly. "It's kind of our specialty."

Lena glanced over her shoulder, her face grim. "You've got what you need?"

Rosy nodded, holding up the encrypted drive. "Everything. Robusco's entire operation is on here."

Zane clapped them on the shoulders. "Good luck. You're going to need it."

Without another word, Jack and Rosy slipped into the shadows, leaving the industrial sector behind. As they disappeared into the Martian night, they couldn't shake the feeling that the hardest part was still ahead of them. But they had the data, and with it, the power to bring Robusco down.

Chapter 21: The Evidence and Escape

Jack and Rosy moved swiftly and silently down the dim corridors of Robusco's complex, the weight of urgency pressing on them like a vice. The alarm echoed in the distance, and their earpieces crackled to life.

"Jack, you're close," Nova's voice said with an edge of tension. "The data vault is three floors down, secure level. You'll need to bypass multiple biometric checkpoints."

Rosy exhaled sharply. "So, no pressure then."

They reached an elevator shaft hidden at the far end of a maintenance tunnel, the doors marked as "Restricted." Jack glanced at Rosy, his face a mask of determination. "Ready?"

She nodded, gripping her equipment tightly. "Let's do this."

The elevator doors opened, and they slipped inside. As they descended, the red emergency lights flashed, bathing their faces in an eerie glow. Each second felt stretched, the weight of their mission hanging heavy between them. They'd prepared for this, but they both knew how little margin for error remained.

The elevator halted, and they stepped into a sterile, cavernous space. Metal doors lined the walls, each secured with biometric locks. At the far end of the hall, a door with reinforced steel plating loomed, its high-tech lock blinking ominously.

"Jack, Rosy," Dr. Orion's voice came through, steady and measured. "That door requires a triple-layer clearance—retinal, fingerprint, and voice."

Jack reached into his bag and retrieved a small device Nova had fashioned, designed to override biometrics with a carefully engineered backdoor code. He slid it onto the lock, holding his breath as the device hummed softly, scanning for any defenses.

A loud beep sounded, and the door slid open.

Inside, rows of holographic screens floated mid-air, each one glowing with scrolling data and complex web maps. This was the heart of Robusco's operation—every shipment, every contact, every clandestine route traced across the solar system.

Jack moved quickly to the central terminal and inserted the data chip Nova had encrypted specifically for this moment. "All right, let's get to work. Rosy, take the client lists. I'll pull the transaction records."

As they worked, screen after screen filled with names, account details, and classified coordinates spanning everything from Earth's orbit to the farthest moons of Saturn. Each line was another piece of evidence, irrefutable proof of Robusco's empire.

Rosy shook her head in disbelief as she skimmed the data. "He's got connections in almost every colony. He's been running black-market shipments of banned tech, even experimental weapons."

Jack's jaw tightened. "Enough to bring him down ten times over."

Outside, footsteps echoed down the hallway. Rosy's head snapped up, her eyes narrowing. "Jack, we've got company."

The footsteps grew louder. Jack and Rosy exchanged a look—they didn't have time to play it safe.

"Nova," Jack hissed into his comm, "we're about to send the data. Can you cover our tracks?"

"Uploading it directly to the encrypted law enforcement network. Just hit send, and I'll handle the rest."

With a few swift commands, Jack and Rosy initiated the upload. The screens flashed as files streamed into the solar system's central authority channels, bypassing Robusco's security systems. Each byte of

BEYOND THE STARS

data sent out waves of evidence, dispersing through encrypted channels where Robusco's grasp couldn't reach.

But as the final files transferred, the vault door flew open. Robusco's guards surged into the room, weapons drawn.

"Stop!" one of them shouted, pointing a blaster at Jack.

Instinctively, Jack pulled Rosy behind him. His eyes darted across the room, searching for an escape route. He felt the adrenaline flood his system, sharpening his senses.

"We're out of options, Jack," Rosy whispered, her face pale but resolute.

Jack raised his hands slowly, trying to stall. "We just wanted to ask Robusco for an autograph," he said with a forced grin.

The guard's eyes narrowed, clearly unimpressed. He signaled to the others to advance.

But Rosy was already a step ahead. She reached into her bag and tossed a small device onto the floor. It detonated with a bright flash, sending the guards reeling backward, their vision temporarily blinded. She grabbed Jack's arm, and together they darted toward a narrow side passage Nova had identified earlier.

"Run!" Rosy urged, half-dragging Jack behind her as the guards recovered, firing blaster shots that echoed off the steel walls.

Dr. Verity's voice came urgently through their comms. "Head down the east corridor; Nova's secured a secondary exit route. You'll have a small window to escape."

They bolted down the passageway, their footsteps pounding in unison. Behind them, the guards were closing in, the sounds of their shouts and gunfire growing louder. Jack and Rosy turned a corner, narrowly dodging a burst of laser fire that seared the wall inches from Rosy's shoulder.

"Keep going!" Jack urged, his own breath ragged as they reached the final door. The small panel beside it blinked green—Nova had overridden the lock just in time.

They stumbled out into the open Martian air, the cold biting through their clothes. Ahead, a small shuttle, provided by Zane and Lena, lay hidden among the rocky terrain. They sprinted toward it, their bodies aching from the exertion and adrenaline. Behind them, the sounds of alarms and shouting guards faded as they threw themselves into the cockpit.

"Strap in!" Jack shouted, fumbling with the controls as he ignited the engines. The shuttle roared to life, and within seconds, they were lifting off, the ground shrinking beneath them.

Rosy leaned back, clutching her side where a blaster shot had grazed her. She winced, her face pale but triumphant. "Did... did it go through?" she managed to ask, her voice faint.

Jack nodded, his own hand clutching a burn on his arm. "The data is out. Every single piece of it."

As they broke free of Mars's atmosphere, the sight of the planet receded below them, a distant red sphere fading into the vast black of space.

Dr. Orion's voice came through their comm, laced with relief. "Jack, Rosy, the transmission was successful. Every major authority from Earth's Interplanetary Council to Saturn's outposts received the data. Robusco's empire will be facing scrutiny on a scale he can't evade."

A small, exhausted smile crossed Jack's face. He glanced at Rosy, their eyes meeting in shared relief and understanding. "We did it."

Rosy let out a weak laugh, her head leaning back against the seat. "So, what now?"

Jack sighed, glancing out at the stars beyond. "We stay under the radar for a while. And maybe, just maybe... we start thinking about what comes next. Together."

Rosy closed her eyes, a faint smile on her lips as they drifted further into the darkness of space, away from the chaos and closer to an uncertain, but hopeful, future.

Chapter 22: Captured

Jack felt the artificial gravity press down on him as their small craft cut silently through the shadowed atmosphere above the base. This isolated outpost on Saturn's frozen moon seemed lifeless from the outside—a weathered dome shielded by titanium plating and thin traces of atmosphere—but beneath its unassuming surface, Jack knew Robusco's true headquarters lay hidden.

Inside the cockpit, Rosy sat beside him, her gaze steady but intense as she scanned the base's perimeter on the ship's small screen. The digital map, provided by Dr. Verity and Nova, highlighted guard stations, surveillance drones, and narrow entry points with which they could bypass the main defenses. Rosy had spent hours studying it, memorizing every detail, and now her practiced fingers glided over the screen, guiding Jack as he maneuvered the ship into an unguarded entry hatch.

"Almost there," Jack whispered. His heart pounded, but he kept his voice steady.

"Let's hope Nova's distraction does its job." Rosy gave him a tight smile before locking her breathing mask in place.

With practiced motions, they adjusted their gear, activated their cloaks, and moved swiftly through the silent corridors of Robusco's fortress. Yet despite the countless hours of planning and perfect timing, their advantage was short-lived. As they rounded a corner near the central command, a sharp buzz filled the air, followed by the loud clang of metal shutters slamming down.

"Welcome to my home," a familiar, cold voice echoed through the corridor. Jack and Rosy froze, exchanging quick glances before they looked up to find a ceiling camera, its blinking red light fixed on them.

Their cover was blown.

A squad of guards, clad in heavy armor, rushed toward them from both ends of the corridor. Jack reached for his blaster, but the guards were faster, pinning his arms before he could raise it. Rosy struggled beside him, twisting and kicking as she tried to fend off her captors, but the guards were relentless, overwhelming them within moments. Before they knew it, both Jack and Rosy were restrained, their wrists bound and blasters taken.

As they were forced forward, the guards roughly guided them down a series of dimly lit hallways. The deeper they went, the more Jack sensed the unsettling presence of Robusco's influence here. The walls were lined with complex weapon systems, crates of forbidden tech, and machines Jack had only ever heard rumors about. It was a chilling reminder of the sheer power Robusco wielded.

Eventually, they were pushed into a vast, open chamber filled with screens, consoles, and a holographic display that flickered with real-time data from every major colony in the solar system. At the room's center stood Robusco, his stance exuding a calm arrogance. He turned as they entered, his lips twisting into a smirk as he looked them over.

"Well, well. The little heroes come knocking on my door." He clasped his hands behind his back, taking slow, measured steps toward them. "I'll admit, you've caused me more trouble than I expected. But I'm curious—did you really think you'd make it out of here alive?"

Jack clenched his jaw, refusing to rise to the bait. "Funny, I was just about to ask you the same thing."

Robusco laughed, a low, mocking sound. "Brave words from someone in restraints." He gestured to the guards, who tightened their grip on Jack and Rosy, forcing them down onto their knees.

"Not so cocky now, are we?" Robusco taunted, his eyes gleaming with malice. "Tell me—what did you hope to accomplish by coming here? Expose me? Destroy my network? I've built an empire across planets, controlled leaders, influenced markets. You're nothing but a minor annoyance."

"You might think that," Rosy retorted, lifting her chin defiantly. "But you're wrong. We've already sent out everything we found. Every law enforcement agency across the system has a copy of your files."

A flicker of irritation crossed Robusco's face, though he quickly concealed it. "And you think that matters?" he replied with a sneer. "Authority means nothing in this game. The people in power are the same people who profit from what I do. It's not justice they're after—it's control. And I'm the one offering it to them."

His gaze turned cold, calculating. "No matter what you've done, you've only succeeded in making yourselves enemies of every influential figure in this system. But maybe you'll be useful to me yet."

Jack felt a chill run down his spine at the implication in Robusco's tone. "You're wasting your breath if you think we'll work for you," he replied.

"Oh, I don't need you to work for me, Jack," Robusco said smoothly. "I just need you to stop meddling."

Jack glanced at Rosy, whose face had gone pale. She met his eyes, and in that silent exchange, he could sense her determination as well as her fear.

Robusco seemed to notice it, his smirk widening. "But I can be merciful," he said in a mockingly gentle tone. "All you have to do is walk away. Go back to your ordinary lives, pretend none of this happened. A small price to pay for survival, wouldn't you agree?"

"Never," Jack said through gritted teeth. "We're going to take you down, one way or another."

Robusco raised an eyebrow, amused. "Very well. Then I guess I'll just have to teach you the consequences of defiance."

He snapped his fingers, and the guards hauled Jack and Rosy to their feet, shoving them toward a side door. They were led down another corridor, this one lined with cells—each containing people who looked half-starved, disheveled, and defeated. As they passed, the prisoners' hollow eyes watched them, a haunting reminder of what awaited them if they didn't find a way out.

Once they were thrown into a cell, the heavy door clanged shut, and Jack and Rosy were plunged into darkness. The only light seeped in from a small, narrow window, casting a dim glow on the cold metal walls.

For a long moment, they sat in silence, catching their breath and absorbing the gravity of their situation. Finally, Jack spoke, his voice a low murmur in the darkness.

"Are you okay?" he asked, reaching out to place a reassuring hand on Rosy's shoulder.

Rosy nodded, though her voice shook. "I will be. But...what now?"

Jack's mind raced, analyzing their options. "We've come this far," he said softly. "And I'm not giving up now. Not after everything we've been through."

Rosy took a deep breath, her voice steadying. "Neither am I. We've made it out of worse situations." She offered him a small, determined smile.

He returned it, finding strength in her resolve. "We'll figure this out. And we'll make sure Robusco pays for what he's done."

As they settled into the uncomfortable silence, Jack began scrutinizing the room. The cell was basic, but he noticed a small access panel along one wall, possibly connected to the base's electrical systems. He turned to Rosy, who caught his look and nodded, understanding what he had in mind.

They shared a silent, resolute determination. No matter how secure Robusco's base seemed, they wouldn't be contained for long. Together, they would find a way out. They had to.

Chapter 23: Face to Face with the Enemy

The air in the room felt thick, almost stifling, as Jack and Rosy were escorted out of the cell and into a cold, metallic chamber. Security drones hovered near the ceiling, casting a dim, ominous light, and the silence was broken only by the distant hum of the base's power generators. The guards, silent and rigid, positioned Jack and Rosy on opposite sides of the room, securing them with restraints that glowed a faint red, indicating their locked status.

In the center of it all, Robusco stood with a self-satisfied smirk, arms crossed as he looked them over. Gone was the mask of professionalism; the man standing before them now was cold, arrogant, and unguarded. His dark eyes gleamed with something almost cruel.

"Well, here we are," he began, his voice soft, almost conversational, though a hint of menace underpinned his words. "Jack, Rosy...two ambitious students from the University of Terra, willing to throw away their lives for what? A misguided sense of justice?"

Jack kept his gaze steady, his face calm, but inside he was battling a simmering rage. Beside him, Rosy's face was set in defiant lines, though he could sense the underlying fear they both shared. Robusco's gaze lingered on them, his expression a twisted blend of amusement and disdain.

"Tell me," Robusco continued, pacing slowly around them. "What made you think you could take me down? Did you really believe your little crusade would lead to anything meaningful?"

Jack clenched his jaw but said nothing, watching Robusco with a mixture of disgust and contempt. The crime lord leaned in, his face a mere inch from Jack's, as if relishing his supposed victory.

"You're nothing more than pawns," he hissed. "Do you even understand what you're up against? My network spans every planet, every moon. I have connections in places you've never even heard of. I've built alliances, brokered deals, and secured loyalties that you couldn't possibly comprehend."

Jack raised an eyebrow, allowing himself a slight smirk. "You sound pretty insecure for a guy who's so 'untouchable.' If you're so powerful, why waste time on us?"

A flicker of irritation crossed Robusco's face before he quickly masked it, his jaw tightening. "Because your interference, however small, has been an annoyance. And I don't like annoyances."

He stepped back, glancing toward Rosy. "And you, Rosy. You've been quite the accomplice, haven't you? Clever, resourceful...maybe even a little dangerous in your own way." His voice dropped to a mocking whisper. "Pity you won't live long enough to see just how insignificant your efforts truly are."

Rosy's eyes flashed with anger, but she kept her tone level. "You're wrong, Robusco. The information we released is already in the hands of the authorities. No matter what you do to us, it's only a matter of time before they come for you."

Robusco laughed, a low, sinister sound that echoed through the room. "Oh, I wouldn't count on that," he said smoothly. "The authorities, as you call them, are as corrupt as anyone. They have their own interests to protect, and believe me, none of them involve shutting down the most profitable network in the system."

"Maybe they're corrupt," Jack shot back, "but we're not. And we're not stopping until you're done for."

Robusco's smile faded, replaced by a cold, calculating glare. "Such determination...foolish, really. But I'll give you one last chance to walk away. Abandon this reckless idealism, and I might consider letting you live."

Jack met his gaze, unflinching. "I'd rather die than let you keep doing what you're doing."

For the first time, Robusco's expression faltered, a flash of genuine irritation breaking through his composure. His fists clenched at his sides as he took a step back, as if trying to maintain control over his growing frustration.

"Well, then," he said, his voice hardening, "you've sealed your own fate."

Jack took advantage of Robusco's momentary lapse in focus, subtly shifting his weight as his eyes scanned the room for anything they could use. His gaze landed on a small device resting on a nearby control panel—likely a data communicator, but with luck, it could create a spark or, at the very least, a distraction.

Rosy caught his gaze, and a subtle exchange of glances passed between them. She took a deep breath, raising her voice in an effort to keep Robusco's attention on her.

"Is this how you measure your success, Robusco?" she taunted, her tone dripping with disdain. "By hiding behind hired guns and secret bases? Seems pretty pathetic for someone who claims to have so much power."

Robusco's face twisted in anger, and he stepped forward, his voice barely controlled. "I've worked too hard and come too far to be undermined by the likes of you," he spat. "You think you're brave, don't you? You think you can change anything?"

Jack seized the moment, reaching out as discreetly as possible to grab the device on the panel. In one swift motion, he activated it, hurling it toward a cluster of electronics by the wall.

There was a sharp burst of light, and the room shook as a small explosion erupted, sending sparks and debris flying. Alarms blared, and smoke began filling the chamber, casting everything in a murky haze.

"Now!" Jack shouted, grabbing Rosy's arm and pulling her toward the exit amid the chaos. The guards scrambled to regain control, but the smoke created just enough cover for them to slip through the confusion.

They ran, Jack leading the way as they navigated the maze of corridors, the alarm echoing around them like a heartbeat. Robusco's furious shouts echoed somewhere behind them, but Jack didn't look back. He focused on moving forward, his grip on Rosy's hand tight as they weaved through the base, evading the guards who had begun to converge on their location.

"Left, here!" Rosy panted, guiding them down a narrow passageway that led toward the base's lower levels. Her mind raced, recalling the schematics Nova had sent them before their mission.

As they reached a stairwell, Jack paused, glancing back down the hallway. Through the haze, he could see shadows moving, the guards hot on their trail.

"We've got to keep moving," Rosy urged, tugging his arm. "We're almost at the auxiliary exit."

Together, they hurried down the steps, each footfall echoing against the cold metal. The air grew colder as they descended, the lights flickering as the smoke reached the lower levels. Finally, they burst into a large, dimly lit hangar, its walls lined with rows of small transport pods.

"Over there," Jack said, pointing to a sleek, unguarded pod at the far end of the hangar. They sprinted toward it, their breaths heavy and labored, as the sounds of approaching footsteps grew louder behind them.

Jack reached the pod first, quickly scanning the controls and activating the ignition. Rosy climbed in beside him, and just as they sealed the hatch, a group of guards appeared at the entrance, raising their weapons.

"Go, Jack!" Rosy shouted, bracing herself as he slammed his hand on the throttle.

The pod lurched forward, engines roaring as it shot toward the hangar's exit. Jack navigated through the narrow opening, the pod's shields shimmering as they deflected the guards' blaster fire. He veered sharply to the right, dodging a barrage of lasers before accelerating into open space.

They sped away from the base, Saturn's ghostly rings glimmering in the distance. The adrenaline still pulsed through Jack's veins, but he allowed himself a moment to glance at Rosy, a breath of relief escaping as he took in her equally relieved expression.

"That was...too close," she murmured, still catching her breath.

Jack nodded, his gaze shifting back to the view in front of them. "But we did it. We got away."

Rosy managed a small, exhausted smile. "And Robusco has no idea what's coming for him now."

Chapter 24: Escape in the Chaos

Smoke billowed and alarms wailed, bathing the metal corridors in a disorienting red light that pulsed with each blare. Jack and Rosy, hearts pounding and breaths ragged, pressed forward through the haze, each step bringing them closer to their chance of escape and freedom. The chaotic scene behind them served as both a cover and a danger, with guards shouting orders and the scent of something burning wafting through the hallways. Jack had no idea what that small device was meant for—it had been a gamble, a last-minute distraction, yet it had worked better than they could have hoped.

"Come on!" Jack urged, glancing over his shoulder. He could barely make out Rosy's figure through the smoke but saw her hand in his, gripping tightly as they moved forward.

"You think Robusco's had enough surprises?" Rosy asked breathlessly, the faintest hint of a grin on her face despite the tension.

"Probably, but I doubt he's done with us just yet."

No sooner had he spoken than Robusco's cold, angry voice crackled through the intercom system, booming across every corner of the base. "Stop them! They're escaping! I want them found now." His voice held a simmering fury that sent a shiver down Jack's spine.

Rosy muttered, "Guess you were right."

They ducked around a corner, blending with the shadows cast by the sporadic emergency lighting. Nova had given them an advantage, providing them with a preliminary map of the base's layout. Still, the corridors looked different under duress, and each corner held the threat of being trapped, especially with Robusco's guards alerted and in pursuit. Jack kept one hand on his compact communicator, watching for Nova's signals to confirm their path.

"Next right," came Nova's metallic voice, calm and steady despite the urgency. "That'll take you to the lift leading to the docking bay."

They turned sharply, finding the lift just as Nova described. Rosy hit the button for the docking bay, and the doors slid shut, but even within the enclosed space, they could hear the rush of footsteps just down the hall. Rosy caught her breath and glanced at Jack, her eyes fierce.

"We're not out of this yet."

Jack nodded, glancing at his communicator as the lift began its ascent. "Keep your guard up. Once we're in the docking bay, it's only a short distance to the escape ships, but Robusco won't make it easy."

The lift doors opened, and a barrage of noise met them—blaring alarms, clashing metal, and footsteps running in every direction. Through the smoke, they could make out ships lining the docking bay, ready for launch. It was as though the entire base had been flipped into survival mode, each person desperately trying to regain control amidst the chaos they had created.

But then, Robusco's voice sounded again. "They're near the docking bay! Do not let them escape!"

Jack gritted his teeth. "We'll have to move fast."

They bolted from the lift, keeping low as they navigated the metal maze of the docking area. As they approached the smaller, less-monitored crafts, a blast sounded behind them. Turning, they saw a group of guards, weapons drawn, advancing with purpose.

"Go, go, go!" Jack urged, firing a few shots behind them to keep the guards at bay.

Rosy led the way to a smaller, inconspicuous craft tucked away in the corner. "Here—it'll be fast, and less likely to attract attention."

BEYOND THE STARS

They scrambled inside, Jack taking the pilot's seat as Rosy engaged the launch systems. The startup sequence was agonizingly slow, and he could feel each second dragging by as another moment Robusco's men had to close in on them. Through the viewport, he could see a group of guards approaching, their weapons raised.

"Just a few more seconds," Rosy muttered, her fingers flying over the controls. "Come on, come on..."

Jack watched the guards, counting down as they raised their blasters. He felt the sweat prickling at his temples. "Any day now, Rosy."

"Got it!" The engines roared to life, and the craft jerked forward, propelling them out of the docking bay and into the expanse of space.

For a moment, relief washed over them—until the sight of pursuit ships emerging from the base brought them back to reality. Jack tightened his grip on the controls, maneuvering the ship with deft precision as the pursuers gained on them.

"Looks like Robusco's not giving up the chase," he muttered, glancing at Rosy, who was monitoring their rear sensors.

Rosy shook her head. "He'll throw everything he has at us to make sure we don't get away." She adjusted the sensor, eyes focused. "There's a clearing through the asteroid belt. If we can lose them in there, we might have a chance."

Jack adjusted the trajectory, setting their course straight for the asteroid field. The asteroid belt loomed ahead, a labyrinth of floating rock and debris that, at such high speed, would challenge even the most experienced pilots. He knew he'd have to focus to avoid a fatal crash.

"Hold tight," he said, the exhilaration mixing with fear as they plunged into the dense field of rocks.

The pursuit ships weren't far behind, navigating the treacherous terrain with skill, but Jack's smaller, nimbler craft allowed them to slip through tighter spaces. Jack made a sharp turn, dodging an asteroid just as it passed, feeling the pull of the inertia as the ship twisted through narrow passages.

"They're still on us," Rosy reported, eyes flicking from the rear sensor to the viewport. "But we're getting some distance."

Jack took another sharp turn, feeling the adrenaline pumping through his veins. The relentless pursuit didn't ease up, but with each evasive maneuver, they gained a few precious seconds of space. Finally, he saw a narrow path through two large asteroids.

"This is it," he said, voice tight. "If they follow us through here, it's going to be close."

Rosy held her breath as Jack plunged the ship between the two massive rocks, the wings barely skimming the edges. A few of the larger pursuit crafts broke off, unwilling to risk the tight space. He saw two ships clip the edge of the asteroid and spin out of control, their fates sealed in moments of reckless pursuit.

Finally, as they cleared the asteroid field, the remaining ships veered off, unable to keep up.

"They're gone," Rosy said, releasing a deep breath. She slumped back in her seat, looking exhausted but relieved. "We did it, Jack. We actually made it out."

Jack couldn't help the small grin spreading across his face as he set the ship on a stable trajectory. He glanced over at her, the adrenaline finally ebbing, replaced by a sense of accomplishment and relief. "We're not out of the woods yet, but Robusco's down a few ships and one big chunk of credibility."

They watched as the distant glow of Saturn's rings passed them by, Robusco's base growing smaller and smaller until it was no longer visible.

"Do you think this will be enough to stop him?" Rosy asked quietly, her voice reflecting the weight of everything they'd been through.

Jack reached over, giving her hand a reassuring squeeze. "We've dealt him a serious blow. And we'll be ready for whatever comes next."

BEYOND THE STARS

With their path clear and the vastness of space before them, they both took a deep breath, bracing for whatever lay ahead. Their mission wasn't over, but for now, they'd escaped the chaos, ready to face the next challenge together.

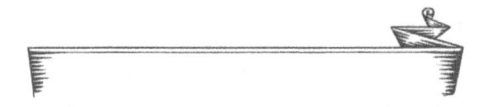

Chapter 25: A Desperate Signal

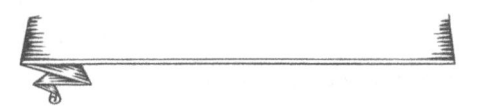

Jack's hand hovered over the control panel, trembling slightly as he struggled to steady his focus. The cramped cockpit was dimly lit, with soft, pulsing lights from the dashboard casting an eerie glow on their faces. Rosy was beside him, her face set with grim determination. Both were battered and exhausted, but they knew there was no turning back now.

"Think this'll work?" Jack's voice was barely above a whisper, a rare hesitation breaking through his usual confidence.

Rosy glanced at him, then at the mess of cables, small devices, and open control panels she'd hastily rigged up. "It has to. I've wired everything I can to boost the signal strength, but we're pushing this poor ship to the edge. One wrong move and the entire system could fry."

"Then let's make it count," Jack said, steeling himself. He leaned over and began inputting the encrypted files they'd managed to extract from Robusco's network. Every piece of evidence they had, every document, transaction, and communication—all of it was now ready to broadcast. It was their last shot at exposing Robusco, and they'd put everything on the line for it.

As Rosy tweaked the final settings, a hum of power surged through the ship. The controls flickered momentarily, and the signal strength monitor spiked. They could see the transmission data begin to upload, slowly, agonizingly slowly, as their small ship fought to keep the systems stable.

Rosy sighed, tension loosening in her shoulders just slightly. "Alright, it's working. The signal's amplifying, but it'll take time."

Jack leaned back, running a hand through his hair, his gaze fixed on the monitor. "Then we wait," he said, though he could feel the unease gnawing at him. They had made it this far, but now, sitting in the silent void of the asteroid belt, it felt like they were exposed, vulnerable. The thought of Robusco intercepting their signal crossed his mind, sending a shiver down his spine.

Minutes turned into an hour, and Jack and Rosy remained on edge. Every beep from the console made them flinch. Jack looked over to see Rosy staring out the narrow viewport, her eyes fixed on the distant stars as though searching for some kind of solace.

"Do you ever wonder what we'd be doing if we hadn't gotten mixed up in all of this?" Jack asked, his voice breaking the silence.

Rosy turned to him, a faint, sad smile crossing her lips. "Sometimes. But if we hadn't... we wouldn't be here. We wouldn't have found all of this out. And who knows what Robusco would be getting away with?" She shrugged, glancing down at the tangled mess of tech she'd cobbled together. "I guess part of me thinks it was always going to be us, one way or another."

Jack nodded slowly, feeling the weight of her words. They were far from the university halls and quiet study rooms where they'd first met, their lives now bound to this mission, to each other.

A small red light on the console began blinking furiously, and the ship shuddered. The signal strength was straining, the ship's outdated systems struggling to keep the transmission flowing.

"Jack, we're losing power on the comms," Rosy said, adjusting the settings to stabilize the system. "It's holding... barely, but we're pushing it."

"Do what you can," Jack replied, reaching out to adjust a few settings himself, hoping they could push through without burning out their only means of communication.

BEYOND THE STARS

The silence was thick between them as they waited, every second dragging out. Rosy's hand drifted toward Jack's, fingers brushing against his in a subtle, unspoken reassurance. For a moment, the fear dissipated, replaced by a fierce determination to see this through, whatever the outcome.

Finally, the console screen beeped again, signaling the transmission had completed. The files had been sent out, scattered across various channels, to every law enforcement agency and media outlet in the system. Now, all they could do was hope someone, anyone, would respond.

Rosy let out a shaky breath, and Jack reached over, squeezing her shoulder. "We did it. No turning back now."

They sat in silence, the realization settling in. But just as relief began to flood their faces, the radar console flickered, emitting a shrill beep. Jack's eyes snapped to the screen. His stomach twisted as he saw several blips appearing on the radar, heading straight for them.

"Jack..." Rosy's voice was barely a whisper, her hand tightening on his arm. She didn't need to say anything more. They both knew what this meant. Robusco's forces had picked up their location, and they were closing in fast.

Jack's mind raced. They were still in the middle of the asteroid belt, and with the ship barely holding together, outrunning Robusco's ships would be nearly impossible. But maybe, just maybe, they could use the belt to their advantage.

"Rosy, buckle in," he said, his voice hardening with resolve. "We're gonna have to get creative."

Rosy nodded, her jaw clenched. She strapped herself in, eyes sharp and focused. "What's the plan?"

"We're going to weave through the asteroid field. It's tight, but if we move fast and stay unpredictable, we might be able to shake them off." He glanced over at her, a spark of fierce determination in his eyes. "Think you can handle it?"

She managed a smile, the fear momentarily replaced with a steely confidence. "If we've come this far, we're not stopping now."

Jack took the controls, pushing the ship to its limit as they dived into the asteroid field. Massive rocks loomed ahead, rotating slowly in the blackness. The ship's engine groaned, but Jack kept a steady hand, navigating with precision. Behind them, the radar showed Robusco's ships closing in, but they were forced to split up, each craft trying to find a clear route through the maze of asteroids.

The seconds stretched into minutes, each turn and swerve demanding everything they had. The ship lurched violently, scraping against a rock, but Jack held firm, adrenaline pumping through his veins. Rosy kept an eye on the radar, calling out directions as Jack maneuvered through the deadly obstacles.

"They're gaining, Jack," Rosy said, her voice taut with tension.

He grimaced, his eyes narrowing as he pushed the throttle. "Then we give them something to dodge."

With a sudden jerk, he angled the ship toward a narrow passage between two enormous asteroids. The gap was barely wide enough for their ship, and Jack could feel the hull scraping as they shot through. Behind them, one of Robusco's ships tried to follow but miscalculated, slamming into the side of the asteroid with a fiery burst.

"One down," Rosy breathed, a hint of relief in her voice. But the radar still showed multiple blips tailing them.

They continued the deadly dance, dodging, weaving, and outmaneuvering as best they could. The asteroid belt seemed endless, the massive rocks closing in around them like silent giants. Just when Jack thought they might have a slim chance, the ship lurched again, a red light flashing on the console.

"Engines are overheating," Jack muttered, gritting his teeth.

"We don't have much longer," Rosy said, her voice tight.

BEYOND THE STARS

A sudden idea sparked in Jack's mind. "Rosy, what if we jettison one of the fuel cells? It'll act as a decoy, and if we time it right, it might explode close enough to damage their ships."

Rosy's eyes widened as she processed the idea. "It's risky, but at this point, we don't have a choice."

With swift, steady hands, she activated the jettison sequence, releasing a fuel cell into the asteroid field behind them. They watched as the blips on the radar drew closer, one of them veering too close to the cell. A second later, a fiery explosion lit up the dark, taking another of Robusco's ships with it.

But two ships remained, undeterred, closing in fast. Jack and Rosy shared a look, bracing themselves for whatever was to come.

Chapter 26: Robusco's Arrival

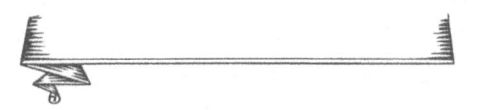

The quiet hum of the cockpit was broken only by the faint, periodic ping of the radar. Jack and Rosy watched the dots on the screen, each blip marking a deadly foe circling ever closer. Their hands were tense on the controls, waiting for the confirmation that they were out of immediate danger. But as Jack studied the radar, a new, ominous shape appeared—a larger, more menacing cruiser moving steadily toward them.

"It's him," Jack murmured, his face growing pale. He clenched his jaw, fingers tapping the console in frustration. "Of course he'd come himself."

Rosy leaned over, eyes widening as she confirmed what he saw. "Robusco. He must be on that ship." Her voice was a mixture of dread and determination. "We knew this would happen eventually, but this… it's like he's bringing everything he has left."

Jack's gaze flickered to her, his expression fierce. "Then we make him pay for it. No way we've come this far to let him take us down now."

The cruiser advanced through the asteroid field, flanked by an entire squadron of sleek, agile fighters. They were far from out of sight, their formation closing in around Jack and Rosy's lone craft. The asteroid belt that had once been their shield now felt like a trap, the rocks that surrounded them confining and unyielding. Jack took a deep breath, hands steady on the controls as he navigated the narrow, twisting paths between the looming asteroids.

"Alright," he said, his voice low but steady. "We use the field to our advantage. If we can keep close enough to the asteroids, they'll have to fly single file and risk collisions. They're bigger, slower. It gives us some leverage."

Rosy's fingers flew over the console as she brought up a 3D map of the asteroid belt. She nodded, marking a path through some of the larger rocks. "I've set the route. It's tight, but if we stick close, we might be able to buy some time before he fully closes in."

Jack nodded. "We'll make it work. Let's go."

As they plunged back into the dense asteroid field, the first shots fired from Robusco's cruiser. The beams cut through the darkness, slamming into nearby rocks and sending chunks of debris spiraling into their path. Jack's heart pounded as he swerved sharply, ducking their ship beneath a massive asteroid just in time to dodge the next volley.

"They're not letting up!" Rosy shouted, gripping the edge of her seat as they careened through a narrow crevice between two hulking rocks.

"Hold on," Jack muttered, gritting his teeth as he expertly maneuvered their craft, skimming the surface of an asteroid that loomed overhead. The cruiser's firepower was relentless, and he felt the ship shudder under the intensity of the blasts nearby. It was clear Robusco wasn't pulling any punches. He was here to end this—permanently.

As they twisted and turned through the labyrinth of stone, Jack noticed Robusco's fighters struggling to keep up. One clipped an asteroid too closely, erupting in a brief, fiery burst behind them. Another tried to follow Jack's evasive maneuvers and misjudged, slamming into a rock that cracked in two, scattering debris in all directions.

But Robusco's cruiser remained close, its heavy firepower outmatching their small ship's agility. With every blast, the distance between them grew narrower, each shot a reminder of just how thin their margin for error had become.

Rosy took a deep breath, scanning the map for an exit route, but their options were running out. "Jack, if we can just get out of the main field, there's a cluster of smaller asteroids near the edge. We might be able to lose them there."

Jack didn't hesitate, shifting their trajectory slightly to make for the outer rim. The field around them grew denser, the rocks closer together. It was a gamble, but one they had to take.

Suddenly, a blast struck the hull of their ship, throwing them sideways. Sparks flew from the control panel, and Rosy yelped as she tried to regain control of the failing systems.

"Damage report?" Jack shouted, wrestling with the controls as he righted the ship.

Rosy glanced down, hands flying over the panel as she assessed the damage. "Shielding's compromised, and we've lost one of the auxiliary thrusters. We're not going to be able to keep this up for long."

Another blast tore past them, close enough to scorch the hull. Jack growled, frustration etched on his face. "Alright, we need to go faster—riskier moves. If we can't keep them off us with speed, we'll have to lose them in the density."

He plunged the ship into a tighter cluster of rocks, dodging left and right as they squeezed through the maze. Robusco's cruiser was forced to slow, but it kept them in its sights, its cannons blazing. Their ship jolted as another shot came dangerously close, skimming their port side.

"They're not stopping, Jack," Rosy said, her voice tight with fear and anger. "This isn't just a pursuit. He's trying to corner us. We have to outsmart him."

Jack nodded, his mind racing. His eyes scanned the field, searching for anything that could give them an edge. Then he saw it—a cluster of smaller, spinning rocks creating a vortex-like pattern just ahead.

He gestured toward it, his voice a mix of hope and desperation. "That vortex—we can lose them in there. Robusco's cruiser is too big to follow us in. If we time it right, the rotation might even shield us."

Rosy's gaze followed his, and she gave a quick nod, adjusting their course. "Alright. But we'll have to be precise. The gravitational pull in there is going to be unpredictable."

Jack didn't waste another second. With a sharp swerve, he angled their ship toward the vortex, accelerating as they neared the cluster of rapidly spinning rocks. Robusco's cruiser hesitated, clearly wary of the vortex, but the fighters continued to press forward, their cannons trained on Jack and Rosy.

As they entered the vortex, the gravitational pull yanked their ship left and right, buffeting them as they navigated the swirling rocks. Jack held his breath, his hands steady on the controls as he timed each twist and turn, narrowly avoiding collisions.

The fighters weren't as fortunate. One by one, they were caught in the swirling rocks, their engines unable to compensate for the vortex's pull. Within moments, the fighters that had been relentlessly pursuing them were gone, destroyed by the very asteroid field they'd tried to use to trap Jack and Rosy.

Jack exhaled a shaky breath, but relief was short-lived. Robusco's cruiser had remained on the periphery of the vortex, watching as his fighters were decimated. Now, it loomed closer, as if waiting for Jack and Rosy to emerge.

"Jack," Rosy whispered, her voice thick with fear. "He's waiting for us. He's not giving up."

Jack's eyes narrowed, and he tightened his grip on the controls. "Then we don't give him the satisfaction. We use what we've got."

With a sudden surge of energy, he redirected power from their remaining shields to the engines, propelling them out of the vortex and directly toward the cruiser. Rosy's eyes widened in shock, but she trusted him, bracing herself for the impact.

BEYOND THE STARS

As they neared the cruiser, Jack veered sharply to the left, angling them toward a narrow gap between the cruiser and a massive asteroid. The cruiser fired, its cannons tearing through the space just behind them. But as they slipped through the gap, the asteroid's gravitational pull forced the cruiser to adjust, slowing it down just enough for Jack and Rosy to pull ahead.

The silence that followed was deafening, broken only by their ragged breaths and the hum of the engine. They'd done it—they'd escaped Robusco's grasp, at least for now.

Rosy looked at Jack, a shaky smile breaking through her fear. "I can't believe we made it. You... you're unbelievable, Jack."

Jack grinned, the adrenaline still coursing through him. "Wouldn't have done it without you, Rosy. Now, let's get out of here before he regroups."

Their ship sped away, leaving the asteroid field behind as Robusco's cruiser grew smaller and smaller in the distance. For the first time in hours, they allowed themselves a moment to breathe, to process the fact that they had survived. But they knew it wasn't over. Robusco was still out there, and their final confrontation loomed closer than ever.

Chapter 27: The Final Stand

Thick clouds of space dust and scattered chunks of rock filled the view outside the cockpit, casting eerie shadows that shifted as Jack piloted the ship deeper into the asteroid field. The landscape was treacherous, a maze of sharp-edged stones and hidden gravitational pulls. But this, Jack thought, was exactly the advantage they needed.

"Alright, this is it," Jack muttered, hands steady on the controls. "We've been running, but now... now we fight."

Rosy took a deep breath, nodding resolutely. "Let's use everything we have. We know this asteroid field better than his forces do. It's our only shot."

For days, they'd barely slept, their only fuel the fierce determination that had brought them here. They'd navigated through the uncharted region of the belt, survived a relentless pursuit, and now, cornered but undeterred, they prepared for the confrontation they both knew was inevitable.

Jack took a quick survey of their weapons systems. They had minimal blasters left and barely enough shielding to survive a direct hit. But the landscape outside their ship—twisting, moving, unpredictable—offered opportunities that blasters alone couldn't.

"Alright," Jack said, his eyes meeting Rosy's. "We set traps in the terrain. There are spots in the field where asteroids move in predictable rotations. We can use that to our advantage, setting up zones where Robusco's ships are forced to enter single file. If we time it right, we can strike at his weak points."

Rosy's gaze sharpened with determination. "And his arrogance... Robusco won't let his men take the risk alone. He'll want to come after us himself."

Jack nodded. "Then we make sure that's the biggest mistake he's ever made."

Over the next few hours, they worked with silent precision, weaving through the asteroids and marking spots that would become their battlefield. They laid explosive charges, reprogramming every device Nova had managed to hack into before Robusco's arrival. Each trap they set was carefully positioned, ready to turn the hazardous environment into a weapon against the massive force on their trail.

Then, finally, it was time. Jack steadied himself at the controls, and Rosy, eyes fixed forward, readied herself for what lay ahead. They had been pushed to their limits—but this was the moment to push back.

Just as Jack activated the first trap, a line of Robusco's fighters emerged from the darkness, their sleek shapes casting shadows against the stars. He counted the ships, each one sliding into position behind Robusco's cruiser, which loomed larger and more menacing than any vessel they'd encountered. Its hull gleamed in the sparse starlight, a silent symbol of the empire Robusco had built on lies, smuggling, and the terror he spread across planets.

A surge of adrenaline shot through Jack's veins. "Here we go."

With a flick of a switch, he detonated the charges on the nearest asteroid cluster. A chain reaction of explosions erupted, sending jagged rock fragments in every direction. The asteroid field lit up in a brilliant, deadly display, forcing Robusco's fighters to scatter. Two fighters broke apart in the blast, and the others had to navigate the deadly debris, their formation splintered.

Jack grinned, gripping the controls tighter. "That's two down. Let's keep it up."

Rosy moved swiftly, her fingers dancing over the console as she activated a hidden mine. Another blast rocked the field, forcing three more fighters to pull away, one of them unable to avoid a sharp turn in time. Its hull crumpled as it crashed into a nearby asteroid, disappearing in a burst of fire.

But the victory was short-lived. Robusco's cruiser powered through, its reinforced shields absorbing the blasts. And as the dust cleared, Jack and Rosy saw the unmistakable glint of Robusco's eyes from the cockpit of his cruiser, his gaze fixed on them with chilling intensity.

"He's coming in himself," Rosy said, her voice barely a whisper.

Jack's heart thudded. "Then it's us and him."

Robusco's voice crackled over the comms, cold and filled with a confidence that seemed unbreakable. "Do you really think your petty little tricks are going to stop me, Jack? Rosy? You're out of your league. You were never a match for me."

Jack smirked, flicking the comms on. "Guess we'll see, won't we?"

As Robusco's cruiser advanced, Rosy activated the ship's last blaster and fired a direct hit toward his left thruster. The blast sparked and exploded, and Robusco's cruiser lurched to the side, momentarily destabilized. The other remaining fighters reformed, but with a sharp turn, Jack maneuvered them deeper into the asteroid field, forcing Robusco to give chase.

The cat-and-mouse game continued, both sides dodging asteroids and stray blasts. But as they maneuvered through one particularly narrow passage, Jack noticed the unmistakable blinking of incoming messages on their distress signal console. A surge of hope shot through him.

"Rosy—look. We got a response!" he shouted, eyes widening as he scanned the readings. "The authorities received our signal. They're close!"

Rosy's face broke into a fierce smile, her gaze never leaving the screen. "We just need to hold him off a little longer. If we can survive this last push... they'll take him down."

Just then, a surge of shots from Robusco's cruiser tore through the shields, and the entire ship jolted as a loud warning blared through the cockpit. Jack and Rosy held on tightly as the ship's systems flickered, the hull groaning under the strain.

"Warning. Shield integrity at critical levels."

The robotic voice echoed in the confined space, and Jack shot Rosy a grim look. "We're not going down like this."

Another blast erupted nearby, and suddenly, the cruiser was on them, its massive form blocking their escape path. Robusco's voice filled the comms again, this time darker and more triumphant. "This is the end of the line for you both. I'm going to enjoy this."

With one final, desperate move, Jack yanked the controls, maneuvering them into the shadow of a massive asteroid. The cruiser followed, but just as it closed in, Jack activated the final explosive charge they'd planted—a charge they had saved specifically for Robusco's ship. A massive blast rocked the entire asteroid, causing it to split and cascade rocks down onto the cruiser, destabilizing it.

Through the smoke and debris, Jack saw the sleek shapes of law enforcement ships piercing through the asteroid field. The authorities had arrived, and with a chorus of sharp commands, they surrounded Robusco's forces.

A grim smile spread across Rosy's face as she met Jack's gaze. "We did it. They're here."

Robusco's cruiser lurched, attempting a desperate retreat. But it was too late. The authorities' ships closed in, lasers trained on his remaining forces. With a final blast, Robusco's cruiser's engines were disabled, leaving him stranded and vulnerable.

Jack exhaled a long, shaky breath as they watched the last of Robusco's empire crumble. After everything they had been through, after every pursuit and narrow escape, it was over.

Rosy looked over at him, her face a mixture of exhaustion and relief. "Jack... it's finally over."

BEYOND THE STARS

He nodded, unable to hide the relief and pride in his own eyes. "Yeah. We actually did it."

As the authorities moved in to arrest Robusco and his men, Jack and Rosy leaned back in their seats, the weight of everything they'd endured settling over them. They were safe, victorious—and finally free.

For the first time in what felt like years, they allowed themselves to breathe, to feel the quiet, incredible relief of victory. And as they looked out at the distant stars, they knew that this was only the beginning of the next chapter in their lives—one they would face together, no longer as fugitives, but as survivors.

Chapter 28: The Last Gambit

Jack's head throbbed as he blinked awake, his vision adjusting to the sterile, harsh light overhead. The cold bite of steel restraints around his wrists and ankles quickly brought him back to reality. Rosy was beside him, bound in a similar chair, her eyes barely open but already filled with a simmering defiance. They'd been captured—again.

"Looks like you finally ran out of tricks, Jack," came a low, menacing voice from across the room.

Robusco's smug figure loomed before them, his arms crossed as he examined his captives. He looked as composed and confident as ever, but there was a flicker of anger in his gaze, a hint of something broken beneath the surface. Perhaps it was the knowledge that his empire was crumbling around him or that Jack and Rosy had come closer than anyone else ever had to toppling his entire operation.

Jack glanced around, trying to get a sense of where they were. The room was small, metallic, and windowless—a holding cell, most likely within Robusco's command ship. Despite the bindings, he leaned forward, giving Robusco a look of absolute defiance.

"So, what now, Robusco?" Jack said, his voice low but strong. "You going to gloat about how you finally got us? Or are you still upset about all those files we leaked?"

A sneer spread across Robusco's face. "Gloating is for the weak. I'm just going to enjoy watching the look on your face when you realize that everything you tried to do was pointless. No one can touch me. You may have scattered some files around, but it's too little, too late.

My connections run deeper than you can imagine. And as for that signal—" He let out a short laugh. "Do you really think help is on the way? They can't save you now."

Rosy managed a small, defiant smile, shaking her head slowly. "You know, Robusco, for a supposed mastermind, you sure underestimate your enemies. That signal we sent wasn't just a call for help. It was everything we had on you. Your routes, your buyers, every shady deal."

Robusco's smile wavered for a split second. His eyes narrowed as he leaned in closer. "You're bluffing."

Jack chuckled, despite the tension of the moment. "Think what you want, but I'd keep an eye on your radar if I were you."

As if on cue, an unexpected alarm blared through the intercom, filling the room with flashing red lights. Robusco straightened, his face darkening as he barked a command to his guards outside. "Status report—now!"

A scrambled reply came through the comms, interspersed with static. "Sir... multiple ships inbound. They're flying the insignia of the Interplanetary Police Force."

Robusco's face fell, his usual confidence faltering as he processed the news. Jack and Rosy exchanged a quick, relieved glance. It had worked. Their signal, their evidence—it had all made it through.

"No, no, no," Robusco muttered, turning away from them as he began to pace the room. He glanced back at Jack and Rosy, his face contorted with a mixture of rage and disbelief. "You... you called them here?"

Jack grinned. "Oh, you'd better believe it. They've got everything, Robusco. And they're not just coming for you. They're coming for every last piece of your network. All of it's over."

For a moment, Robusco was silent, his expression unreadable. Then, with a sudden surge of fury, he reached into his coat and drew a sleek blaster, aiming it directly at Jack.

BEYOND THE STARS

"You think I'll just let you sit here and watch it all fall apart?" he hissed, his voice trembling with anger. "No. I'm going to end this on my terms."

Rosy tensed, her eyes darting from the blaster to Robusco's face. "You think killing us is going to change anything? They're still coming for you, Robusco. You're finished."

Robusco smirked, but his confidence looked strained. "I've rebuilt from worse."

He raised the blaster, his finger tightening on the trigger, but a sudden impact shook the entire room. The lights flickered, and a voice came over the loudspeaker.

"This is Commander Lyra Tanis of the Interplanetary Police Force. We have your ship surrounded, Robusco. Power down your weapons and surrender, or we'll breach by force."

Jack couldn't help the grin that spread across his face. "Sounds like the cavalry's here."

Robusco cursed under his breath, his gaze darting around as he weighed his options. The reality of his situation was sinking in, and his grip on the blaster wavered slightly.

With his attention momentarily diverted, Jack saw his chance. He leaned forward, straining against his bindings just enough to press the heel of his boot against the edge of his chair, feeling for the small compartment he'd managed to open earlier. With a flick of his foot, a slim, sharpened tool slipped into his hand—one of the few small gadgets he and Rosy had managed to conceal.

Working quickly, he began to saw at the restraints around his wrists, keeping his eyes fixed on Robusco, who seemed too lost in his own thoughts to notice. Rosy caught on, giving Jack the smallest nod of encouragement.

"You can't win this, Robusco," Rosy said, her voice deceptively calm, drawing his attention back to her. "Surrender, and maybe they'll go easy on you."

Robusco scoffed. "You think I'm afraid of some interplanetary police force? I own half of them."

But as if in direct contradiction, another violent tremor rocked the ship. A voice from the comms shouted, "Sir, they're breaching the main hull!"

The look on Robusco's face turned from anger to panic. In that moment of distraction, Jack felt the last of his bindings snap free. Without hesitation, he lunged forward, grabbing Robusco's wrist and twisting it, forcing the blaster out of his hand. The weapon clattered to the floor, and Rosy managed to kick it out of reach.

Before Robusco could react, Jack pinned him against the wall, his face inches away. "Game over."

Robusco glared, his breath coming in shallow gasps, but he couldn't deny the truth of Jack's words. The unmistakable sound of boots echoed in the corridor, followed by the sharp commands of law enforcement officers moving through the ship. Jack kept his hold on Robusco, his gaze steady.

The door to the cell burst open, and Commander Lyra Tanis strode in, flanked by two armed officers. She glanced at Jack and Rosy, giving them a nod of acknowledgment, before turning her gaze to Robusco with an icy glare.

"Robusco," she said, her voice carrying a cold authority, "you're under arrest for interstellar smuggling, bribery, and numerous counts of illegal trafficking. It's over."

Robusco's shoulders sagged, the last of his resistance crumbling as the officers stepped forward, placing cuffs around his wrists. He didn't look at Jack or Rosy as they led him from the room, but Jack saw the haunted look in his eyes—the realization that, for once, his power couldn't save him.

As the door closed behind them, Jack and Rosy shared a moment of silence, letting the weight of everything settle over them. They'd done it. Robusco's empire was finished, and justice was finally being served.

Commander Tanis approached them, her expression softening. "We received your signal—everything you sent was invaluable in building the case against him. The galaxy owes you two a debt of gratitude."

Jack smiled, nodding in acknowledgment. "Thanks, Commander. But honestly, we're just glad it's over."

Tanis tilted her head, a hint of a smile playing on her lips. "Something tells me this is just the beginning for you two. People with your courage don't just fade into the background."

Rosy chuckled, exchanging a knowing glance with Jack. "Maybe. But right now, I think we could both use some time somewhere quiet. Just for a while."

Commander Tanis nodded. "You've earned it."

As they made their way off the ship, the weight of everything that had happened began to lift, replaced by a profound sense of relief. The future was uncertain, but for the first time in a long time, they felt truly free. They'd faced down an empire, taken on impossible odds, and emerged victorious. Whatever lay ahead, they knew they'd face it together.

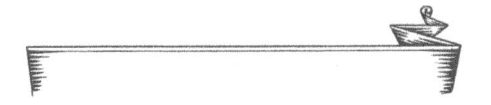

Chapter 29: A Hero's Welcome

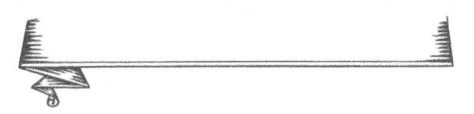

The ship hummed softly as it approached Earth's orbit, the familiar blue and green planet swelling in the viewport. Jack leaned back in his seat, the fatigue of the past days etched across his face, while Rosy sat beside him, staring down at their home world, a faint smile on her lips. They shared a glance, the weight of their journey easing in that moment as Earth's expanse stretched out below, bringing them back to familiar ground and, finally, to safety.

"I never thought I'd miss these skies so much," Jack murmured, his voice tinged with relief.

"Me neither," Rosy replied, placing a reassuring hand on his arm. "Feels surreal, doesn't it? Like... did all that really happen?"

Jack laughed, the sound bubbling up unexpectedly. "I keep waiting to wake up and realize we just crammed too hard for some history exam." He shook his head, the corners of his mouth turning up as he glanced over. "Guess that explains why I'm so tired."

They were soon interrupted by a comm chime, followed by a message from the ship's AI, notifying them that they were approaching the central spaceport. The ship shifted, aligning itself with the entry protocols, and as it did, Jack's mind drifted back to the moment authorities had swarmed Robusco's asteroid base. He remembered the wild panic, the mad scramble as they'd finally captured Robusco, who had looked as stunned as they had been relieved. Even now, it felt like something out of a dream.

The ship's landing gear settled on the platform with a soft thud, and Jack and Rosy exchanged a look, both knowing that this moment was the first step back into normalcy. But as the door to their shuttle opened, the cheers outside were anything but normal.

The two stepped out, blinking in surprise at the throng of people waiting just beyond the security clearance area. Journalists, government officials, students—they were all there, holding signs and snapping photos. Rosy turned to Jack, eyes wide, and whispered, "Did... did they do all this for us?"

It wasn't long before Dr. Carson was there, pushing through the crowd, her face split into a wide grin. She reached them, pulling them into a hug, her energy almost sweeping them off their feet. "You did it!" she exclaimed, tears glistening in her eyes. "You two changed everything."

"Dr. Carson," Jack managed, barely able to believe she was standing there, beaming at them, "I... we wouldn't have been able to do it without you. And the others—Dr. Verity, Dr. Orion, Nova... They're the real heroes."

"Oh, don't you start trying to be humble now," Dr. Carson chuckled, her voice warm. "Everyone in the solar system knows your names now. Jack, Rosy, you've shone a light on something that no one else could."

Rosy was still taking it all in, her expression dazed as she gazed around. "Did... did people really know? That we were out there, risking everything?"

Dr. Carson placed a steady hand on her shoulder. "Yes. And they're thankful. The broadcasts picked up your distress call after all. People were rallying for you all across the planets. The authorities couldn't ignore it. By the time they arrived to capture Robusco, his whole empire was crumbling from within."

Jack let out a deep breath, feeling as though a weight he'd carried for ages had finally lifted. The long nights, the relentless escapes, the fights—it all seemed worth it now, seeing the relief and hope in the faces of those around them.

Soon after, they were whisked away by the officials, taken to a secure briefing area where several high-ranking members of the interplanetary law force waited. They spent hours recounting their journey in detail, sharing every recorded bit of evidence they'd gathered and re-examining the data that had finally brought down Robusco's network.

One officer, a tall man with a crisp uniform and an approving smile, shook their hands as the briefing ended. "It's an honor, really. What you've done here isn't just the takedown of one smuggler—it's the beginning of a safer, fairer system. People like Robusco depended on secrecy and power, and you exposed both."

As the officials left, Jack and Rosy sat alone for a moment, the quiet finally wrapping around them like a blanket. "So, what now?" Jack asked, his voice softened, almost cautious as if he couldn't quite believe it was over.

"Well..." Rosy began, tilting her head thoughtfully. "Maybe we'll take a long, very long vacation." She laughed, leaning her head on his shoulder. "Or maybe we'll stay close to the stars. Because, you know, they're a little brighter now."

They exchanged a look, a shared understanding passing between them. The stars, the moons, the vast stretches of the solar system—they held memories of their fight, their bravery, and the bonds they had built, not just with each other but with everyone who had risked everything for justice.

Dr. Carson soon rejoined them with a message, a broad grin on her face as she held out two sleek, official-looking badges, emblazoned with the interplanetary law force insignia. "How about a permanent position with us? As consultants, of course. We could use bright minds like yours, especially ones with your experience."

Jack looked at Rosy, who raised an eyebrow, her eyes twinkling. "Back to the front lines?" she asked him with a smile.

He grinned, reaching out to accept the badges from Dr. Carson. "Well, it looks like we might just be getting started."

As they left the building and stepped back into the crowd, they found themselves looking up, the stars still gleaming in the night sky. Earth's lights stretched below them, but all Jack and Rosy could think of was the promise of the galaxies that lay beyond, and the adventures that still awaited.

With hands clasped and minds open to what lay ahead, they turned, each step taking them forward into the vast unknown, together.

Chapter 30: A New Beginning

Jack and Rosy stood on the observation deck of their ship, gazing out into the vastness of space. The stars stretched endlessly before them, each one a pinprick of light in the dark void, inviting them into its mysteries. The weight of their journey, the harrowing battles, and the bittersweet victory they'd just won still hung in the air, but it felt lighter now. The universe was finally quiet, and for the first time in months, they allowed themselves a deep breath.

Jack broke the silence first, his voice soft, thoughtful. "It's strange, isn't it? Just a few months ago, all we could think about was finishing university and maybe finding a decent job. And now..."

Rosy's lips curved into a small smile. "And now we're outlaws turned heroes with half the solar system talking about us. Not exactly what we had in mind, was it?"

They shared a laugh, the sound echoing through the otherwise silent deck. For a moment, it was just them, standing shoulder to shoulder, the remnants of the battles they'd faced lingering in their expressions but beginning to fade.

Jack turned to her, his eyes warm. "Rosy, I can't imagine doing any of this without you. Not the missions, not the narrow escapes...not even the terrifying parts. Especially not the terrifying parts."

Rosy looked down, her cheeks warming. "Neither can I, Jack. I think...maybe it was always meant to be this way. Like we were supposed to meet. Supposed to go through all this." She paused, glancing back out the window. "I just don't know what we're supposed to do next. Do we go back? Do we stay out here, in the stars?"

Jack took a deep breath, considering. "Maybe we don't have to know yet." He stepped closer, reaching out and taking her hand. "What if we just... see where the universe takes us?"

Rosy laughed, shaking her head. "You make it sound so easy."

"Why not? It doesn't have to be complicated. We've been running on a schedule for so long, it feels strange to think of just...choosing where we go next. Together. As partners."

At his words, Rosy turned to look at him fully, searching his face. She'd felt this bond between them grow through every crisis, but hearing him say it—calling them partners in a way that was unmistakably deeper than just their shared mission—made her heart race.

"Jack," she whispered, "Are you saying...?"

He nodded, squeezing her hand. "Yeah. I'm saying exactly that. We've faced so much together, Rosy. I want to see what else is out there with you, wherever that may lead."

Tears stung her eyes, and she smiled, holding his hand tightly. The weight of their experiences seemed to dissolve, leaving only hope and excitement in its place.

They stood together in silence for a while longer, watching the stars. After a moment, Rosy spoke up, her tone playful. "So, where do you think we should go first, Captain?"

Jack grinned, leaning against the rail beside her. "Well, I heard Saturn has some spectacular views. We could start there. Or maybe one of those moons we kept passing by during all the missions. Who knows? The galaxy's wide open now."

Rosy tilted her head, considering. "I like the sound of that. But maybe...just this once, we take a break. No missions, no chases, just...us. A real adventure, but on our own terms."

BEYOND THE STARS

He chuckled, wrapping an arm around her shoulders and pulling her close. "Agreed. Our next mission will be for us, wherever it leads."

They stood there, wrapped in each other's warmth, letting the calm of the stars fill the silence. They had come so far, faced so much, and through it all, they'd found each other. They were no longer just Jack and Rosy, two students trying to find their place in the universe—they were something stronger, something bound by shared battles and unspoken promises.

With one last look at the stars, Jack pulled her in for a soft, lingering kiss. When they finally parted, he smiled, his eyes full of love and excitement.

"Here's to new beginnings," he murmured, and Rosy smiled back, her eyes shining with the same excitement.

"New beginnings," she echoed, her heart racing with the possibilities.

Hand in hand, they turned away from the observation deck, ready to face whatever lay ahead, knowing that, together, they could face anything. The stars would be their guide, and the universe, in all its vast mystery, lay open before them.

For Jack and Rosy, this was only the beginning.

Terminology for *Beyond The Stars*

1. StellarNet

The primary communication network used across the solar system. StellarNet provides instantaneous communication, essential for interplanetary messages, research, and information sharing, while also being closely monitored by planetary authorities to prevent misuse.

2. Warp Routes

Specially designated space pathways that allow faster-than-light travel between planets. Though well-patrolled by authorities, these routes are occasionally exploited by smugglers like Robusco to move illegal goods between planets undetected.

3. Interplanetary Law

A unified legal framework that governs conduct across all human-occupied planets and moons, aimed at promoting peace and safety throughout the solar system. It's enforced by a specialized police force known as the Interstellar Authority.

4. The Interstellar Authority (ISA)

The solar system's primary law enforcement agency, tasked with maintaining order across colonies and space routes. ISA agents are highly trained and armed with advanced technology, often working undercover to catch high-level criminals.

5. Rogue Zones

Unmonitored or remote regions within the solar system, often rich in asteroids and rare minerals. These zones attract smugglers and fugitives, making them notorious hideouts for illegal activity. Jack and Rosy encounter one such zone in the asteroid belt, where they are forced to make a stand.

6. AI Professors

Advanced artificial intelligence systems programmed to serve as educators in universities, providing knowledge, mentorship, and resources to students. These professors, like Dr. Verity and Dr. Orion, are crucial allies, offering vast informational access and real-time strategic support.

7. Solar Credits

The universal currency used across human-inhabited planets. Solar Credits are a digital form of currency, easily transferred across distances, but prone to illegal transactions on the black market.

8. Data Vaults

Highly secure storage facilities used by corporations and criminals alike to store sensitive information. Robusco's vault, located deep in his Mars headquarters, holds the key to his smuggling network and client list.

9. AstroCraft

Specialized spacecrafts equipped for long journeys, often fitted with warp drive engines. Jack and Rosy use an AstroCraft to navigate both civilized routes and rogue zones, essential for their evasive maneuvers and survival.

10. Nova

The alias of a mysterious hacker who specializes in interplanetary data breaches. Known for targeting criminal organizations, Nova aids Jack and Rosy by providing information on Robusco's network and crafting escape strategies.

11. Martian Outposts

Remote, fortified locations on Mars where smugglers and other criminals operate under the radar. Robusco's operations heavily rely on these outposts, which are difficult for ISA to monitor closely due to Mars's complex terrain.

12. Stellar Shields

Defense systems installed on spacecrafts to repel attacks. While not impervious, these shields provide critical protection in hostile encounters, allowing ships to withstand blasts and minor collisions.

13. Oxygen Synthesizer

A standard-issue device used in space suits and AstroCrafts to produce breathable air, especially necessary for survival in rogue zones and prolonged missions.

14. Lunar Protocols

A specialized code of conduct for operations on moons, outlining strict guidelines for resource extraction, environmental preservation, and human safety. Some moons enforce these protocols rigorously, while others—like Robusco's hideout—are more lax, allowing criminal activity to thrive.

15. Deep Space Comms (DSCs)

High-powered, long-range communicators capable of sending distress signals or other data across vast distances. Jack and Rosy rely on a DSC to broadcast their evidence, hoping to reach the ISA despite being in a remote area of the asteroid belt.

---

16. Quantum Relays

Specialized communication nodes that boost signal strength across vast distances. Quantum Relays allow for nearly real-time communication between planets and are strategically placed along warp routes to maintain a stable network.

17. HoloDecks

Advanced virtual reality chambers that recreate environments for training, simulations, and relaxation. Jack and Rosy use a HoloDeck to prepare for their infiltration missions, practicing maneuvers and escape tactics in simulated versions of enemy bases.

18. Grav-Lock Boots

Footwear technology that allows wearers to magnetically adhere to surfaces, especially useful in low-gravity or zero-gravity environments. Essential for movement within asteroid fields or inside spacecraft with varying levels of gravity.

19. ExoSuits

Specialized suits worn for protection in hostile environments, such as extreme cold, heat, or vacuum. ExoSuits come with built-in oxygen tanks, radiation shielding, and nano-fiber armor, giving users extra protection during risky missions in space.

20. NeuroLink Implants

Optional cerebral implants used to enhance memory retention and cognitive speed. Some agents and high-level operatives have these installed for quick data processing, though there are ethical concerns around misuse.

21. Nebula Gas Mining

The process of extracting valuable gases from nebula regions. Often risky due to unstable conditions, nebula gas mining attracts both legitimate companies and black-market operators. Robusco is rumored to profit from black-market nebula mining.

22. Holo-Messaging

A communication method where messages are sent in holographic form, allowing for more immersive interactions. Jack and Rosy receive urgent updates from Nova and the professors via holo-messages, providing real-time tactical advice during missions.

23. Spectra Scanners

High-precision scanning devices capable of detecting hidden compartments, life forms, and weapons on ships or structures. Jack and Rosy frequently use Spectra Scanners to assess threats and locate hidden data caches during infiltration.

24. Nano-Healers

Tiny robotic medical devices that can quickly repair tissue, stop bleeding, and treat minor injuries. Nano-Healers are a critical part of space travel, where access to hospitals is limited, and they aid Jack and Rosy in recovering after close encounters.

25. Ion Cannons

High-powered weapons mounted on Robusco's cruiser, capable of immobilizing smaller ships. Ion Cannons discharge charged particles that disable ship systems, making them a constant threat to Jack and Rosy's escape plans.

26. Phase Cloak

An advanced cloaking device that temporarily renders ships invisible to detection systems. Although highly illegal, these are used by high-level smugglers. Robusco's base is rumored to have a Phase Cloak, making it nearly undetectable to the ISA.

27. Stellar Medals

The highest honor awarded by the Interstellar Authority for exceptional bravery and service across planetary borders. Jack and Rosy's actions could earn them this rare recognition, celebrated throughout the solar system.

28. SolarCraft Base

A specialized hub for spacecraft maintenance and repairs, typically located near major planetary trade routes. Many SolarCraft Bases have become key checkpoints for authorities searching for smugglers, forcing people like Robusco to rely on remote outposts instead.

29. CryoPods

Capsules used for suspended animation during long space journeys. CryoPods slow the body's metabolic rate, allowing travelers to safely sleep through lengthy trips, especially useful for undercover agents or deep-space explorers.

30. Zero-G Combat

A specialized form of combat training designed for use in zero-gravity environments. Jack and Rosy rely on their Zero-G Combat skills when maneuvering around asteroids and evading Robusco's men in the hostile terrain of outer space.

31. Plasma Blades

Handheld weapons that emit a controlled plasma arc, useful for both combat and cutting through metal surfaces. Jack and Rosy utilize Plasma Blades in tense confrontations, and these tools prove invaluable in escape situations.

32. AstroNav

A navigational AI system embedded within spacecrafts, capable of calculating warp routes, identifying asteroid paths, and pinpointing safe docking locations. Jack and Rosy's AstroNav helps them outmaneuver Robusco in the asteroid belt.

33. Comet Dust Protocols

Safety guidelines for navigating through comet trails, which contain high-velocity particles and radiation hazards. These protocols are essential for any ship entering comet zones, adding a layer of danger to the rogue routes Jack and Rosy must take.

34. Intergalactic Trade Agreement (ITA)

An agreement between inhabited planets regulating trade, taxation, and anti-smuggling measures. The ITA enforcement is a challenge, but it serves as the basis for the Interstellar Authority's pursuit of criminals like Robusco.

35. Celestial Market

The informal name for the underground trade network spanning the solar system, where high-value goods, banned substances, and advanced tech are sold. Robusco's empire thrives here, evading detection by the ISA.

36. Omega Drive

A highly encrypted storage device that contains classified or sensitive information. Robusco's Omega Drive holds vital data on his operations, making it one of Jack and Rosy's primary targets during their infiltration.

37. Gravity Wells

Areas of intense gravitational pull, commonly found near large asteroids or planetary bodies. Gravity Wells pose serious risks to spacecraft, and Robusco's forces often use them as tactical traps against intruders.

Don't miss out!

Visit the website below and you can sign up to receive emails whenever Anupam Roy publishes a new book. There's no charge and no obligation.

https://books2read.com/r/B-A-UKBS-QQSFF

BOOKS 2 READ

Connecting independent readers to independent writers.

Did you love *Beyond The Stars*? Then you should read *Selected Halloween Stories*[1] by Anupam Roy!

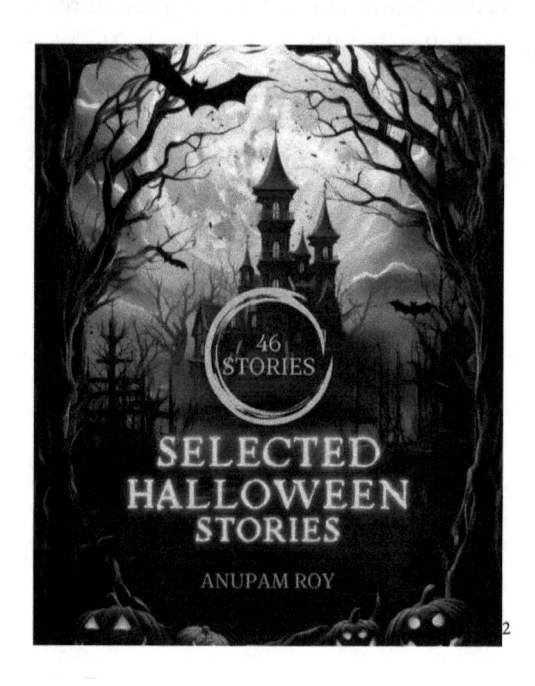

Selected Halloween Stories is a spine-tingling anthology that brings together 46 tales of mystery, magic, and the supernatural, perfect for celebrating the thrill of Halloween. From lighthearted mischief to bone-chilling hauntings, this collection captures the many faces of the season where the veil between worlds is at its thinnest.

Featuring stories from four unique collections—*The Midnight Masquerade*, *The Dance of the Undead*, *The Archivist's Curse*, and *Ghost Stories*—this book takes readers on a journey through eerie adventures, ghostly encounters, and supernatural surprises. Explore tales of haunted houses that hide dark secrets, magical clocks that whisk trick-or-treaters through time, and enchanted candy that brings more

---

1. https://books2read.com/u/3GJKpp

2. https://books2read.com/u/3GJKpp

than just sweetness. Each story offers its own twist, blending humor, romance, and a touch of fright to create a mix of the eerie and the enchanting.

Whether you're looking for a playful escape into a world of mischievous spirits or a chilling dive into the shadows, ***Selected Halloween Stories*** has something for every Halloween lover. So light a candle, settle in, and prepare for a bewitching night of storytelling where anything is possible, and every page brings a new kind of magic.

Also by Anupam Roy

American Heroes
The Heroes of American Freedom Movements: A Glimpse of American History

A Study in Scarlet: Annotated
Sir Arthur Conan Doyle's A Study in Scarlet: Annotated

Christmas Story Time
Christmas Stories
Christmas Stories
Christmas Stories Volume 3

Galactic Nexus Series
Beyond The Stars

Ghost Stories
Ghost Stories

The Archivist's Curse
The Midnight Masquerade
The Dance of the Undead

Greek Mythology
Greek Mythology, Volume 1

Greek Mythology: A Teen's Version
Greek Mythology: A Teen's Version

Happy Easter Story Anthology
Happy Easter Volume 1
The Easter Bunny's Secret
Chronicles of The Easter Bunny

I'm Maya And It's My Story
I'm Maya And It's My Story

The Adventures of Alex Mercer
The Midnight Mansion Mystery

The Adventures of Zoro
The Adventures of Zoro: The Rise of North Brook

The Toy Kingdom
The Toy Kingdom Volume 1
The Toy Kingdom Volume 2
The Toy Kingdom Volume 3

The Toyoearth
The Toyoearth Volume 1

Valentine's Day Love Stories
Valentine's Day Love Stories Volume 1
Valentine's Day in Venice
The Love Locket
Chasing Fireflies

Valentine's Day Mystery Anthology
Love's Mysterious Embrace
Roses and Riddles
Enigmatic Hearts

Warrior Chronicles
Napoleon Bonaparte: The Enigma Unveiled
Alexander
Joan of Arc: Unveiling the Untold Secrets

Standalone
How to Increase Confidence and Be Successful
Unlock Your True Potential
A Comprehensive Guide to Yacht Maintenance
✧✧✧✧ ✧✧✧✧ - Towards Light
Unlock the Secret to the Most Magical Christmas Ever! Unique Celebrations Await!
New Year Resolutions: Look Before You Leap
Christmas Stories Omnibus
New Year, New You: A Holistic Approach to Personal Growth
Financial Fitness for the New Year
The Wealth Mindset Blueprint
Valentine's Day Love Stories
Happy Saint Patrick's Day
Happy Easter Story Anthology
The Last Supper
From Startup to Scaleup: The Entrepreneur's Playbook for Growth and Impact
The Stories on St. George's Day
The Symphony of the Sea
The Beat of Our Hearts
Forbidden Juneteenth Love
The Story of American Independence: A Journey to Freedom
The Power of Action: Unlocking the Path to Success
The Long Game
The Bluebone Pirates
The Empire of the Sun: An Incan Chronicle
The Dawn of the Jaguar
Cleopatra
Halloween Omnibus
Selected Halloween Stories

About the Author

Anupam Roy, born on January 6, 1982, in the serene town of Kalna, Burdwan district, West Bengal, India, is a distinguished poet and author based in Murshidabad, near Kolkata, in India. His academic journey led him to the esteemed University of Burdwan, where he pursued a Master of Arts in English, a discipline that would become the canvas for his storytelling.

Literature is Anupam Roy's first love, and it serves as his medium for connecting with the human experience and delving into the intricate tapestry of human emotions. He has authored numerous books, each a testament to his literary prowess and his ability to encapsulate the essence of human existence. His writing is characterized by lyrical beauty, evocative imagery, and keen observation, often transforming everyday moments into poetic expressions that explore the complexities of human relationships.

Beyond his literary pursuits, Anupam Roy is a revered figure in West Bengal's literary circles and beyond. His work transcends cultural boundaries, resonating with readers from diverse backgrounds, a testament to the universality of his themes and the depth of his insights.

Anupam Roy's writing often delves into the profound connection between nature and human existence, celebrating the beauty of the natural world while exploring the depths of human emotions. His eloquent words and poignant storytelling continue to inspire and captivate readers, leaving an indelible mark in the world of Indian literature.

An ongoing exploration of the human condition, Anupam Roy's literary journey invites readers to embark on a voyage of self-discovery and reflection through the power of literature. His ability to convey life's complexities in simple yet profound terms solidifies his status as a cherished figure in Indian literature, touching the hearts and minds of those privileged to read his work.

Milton Keynes UK
Ingram Content Group UK Ltd.
UKHW022019131124
451149UK00013B/1203